# *The Bad Boy Billionaire's Wicked Arrangement*

**Also by Maya Rodale**

*The Wicked Wallflower*
*Three Schemes and a Scandal* (Novella)
*Seducing Mr. Knightly*
*The Tattooed Duke*
*A Tale of Two Lovers*
*A Groom of One's Own*

# *The Bad Boy Billionaire's Wicked Arrangement*

MAYA RODALE

AVONIMPULSE
*An Imprint of HarperCollinsPublishers*

EPub Edition JANUARY 2014 ISBN: 9780062230812

Print Edition ISBN: 9780062230829

JV 10 9 8 7 6 5 4 3

*For Tony . . . this romance novelist's*
*very own startup hero*

## *Acknowledgments*

I'd like to thank Molly Graham, Amanda Kimble-Evans, Heewa Barfchin, and Katharine Ashe for reading early drafts of this manuscript and providing invaluable feedback. Thank you to Daniel for reviewing the lines of Javascript that appear in this story. I am especially indebted to Tony Haile for introducing me to the tech world, reading numerous versions of this book, helping me plot, and encouraging me to learn how to code. Thanks, Baby!

## *Chapter One*

```
$(document).ready(function() {
```

*New York Public Library*

*@DukeAusten: I'm at New York Public Library (New York, NY) http://4sq.com/1771KOK #HushParty*

As THE FUTURE Mrs. Sam Chase, I never went to glamorous and raucous New York City parties like this. It was no place for the likes of me: a girl who had planned on a life of Vera Wang Blanc Sur Blanc china patterns, baby names straight from most-popular list, and a house on leafy Brook Street in the town where Sam and I, high school sweethearts, had grown up, fallen in love and planned to live happily-freaking-after.

Plans. Ha.

These days I was just Jane, jilted Jane, on my own and

out of place at this mad crush of a party, an event known as The Hush Party, hosted by the gossip website Gawker.com.

By day I worked here in the New York Public library as Library Assistant.

But tonight . . .

The reading room on the top floor had been taken over by a thousand fashionable, pretty young things. Under soaring ceilings and arched windows overlooking the breathtaking city skyline, a string quartet played Vivaldi. But everyone was dancing to thumping club music broadcast only through the wireless headphones everyone wore.

Civilization, meet debauchery.

It was like two different parties under one roof. I didn't quite belong to either of them.

I stood above it all on the narrow balcony that lined the room. Behind me, a wall of books. Before me, a delicate iron railing that seemed insufficient restraint. I watched people dance to the club music pumping through their headphones. Heads were bopping and hips were shaking in time to a beat that I was deaf to. Arms were waving in time to a song I couldn't hear. Drinks in hand, people danced wildly where students usually studied in silence at long tables.

Nearly everyone wore black domino masks. One had been handed to me when I arrived with my friend and roommate, Roxanna, but I had lost her in the crowd. I felt too foolish to wear it on my own.

Like a wallflower, I hovered, watching the party unfold around me. Present but not a part of it. My fingers twitched around the mask. If only I dared to put it on. I wore the headphones around my neck and felt the vibrations of the bass thumping against my collarbone. If only I dared . . .

I took a sip from my glass of champagne and felt a twinge of guilt. The sign said, "NO CAMERAS, FOOD OR BEVERAGES IN THE READING ROOM." I was not in the habit of breaking the rules. Ever.

Except for tonight.

Where had being good gotten me anyway?

I took another, small defiant sip of the champagne. My gaze once again settled on a certain guy. I couldn't figure him out no matter how often I glanced at him from my perch on the balcony. He was dressed down in a grey fitted T-shirt and dark jeans. His hair was a tousled mess, his jaw was strong and unshaven. It was nearly midnight, but he looked like he'd just rolled out of bed.

I easily imaged him as one of the pirates and rogues I read about in historical romance novels. It wasn't just how he looked, either, but the way he moved through the crowd. Really, the man *swaggered*. Everyone turned to greet him. He grinned, shook hands firmly, and laughed. The girls gave him flirtatious smiles followed by longing glances as he passed them by.

Obviously, he belonged here. Obviously, he was SOMEONE.

I had no idea who. Roxanna, my roommate and writer of gossip and salacious tales for the website Jezebel.com would surely know. While she had gotten me into the party, I'd lost track of her hours ago.

I strolled along the balcony, following that guy with

my eyes, and tracing my fingers along the spines of all the leather volumes of old encyclopedias and other reference books. I didn't quite belong *here* but Sam had made it clear I didn't belong with him anymore, either.

I had been expecting a proposal and I had gotten dumped instead, all because I was the kind of girl who didn't wear the mask, the kind of girl who felt guilty about drinking champagne in the library, the kind of girl who didn't break the rules. The kind of girl who *didn't.*

I had moved to New York City to escape all that. Yet here I was, clinging to the shadows, hovering around the perimeter of the room like a prim spinster. That wasn't who I wanted to be.

That guy happened to glance up my way. Our gazes locked from across the room. His eyes were dark and intently focused on me. It went to my head, that look, and silenced sense and reason.

I swallowed the rest of my champagne.

I put on the mask.

And then I followed that guy.

AND THEN I wished I hadn't.

Black mask over my eyes, I slid into the crowd trying to make my way through as they pushed and pulsed against me. I lost him, but managed occasional glimpses when the crowd parted.

I saw him push through double doors leading to the rare books room, a small, cozy chamber that was usually off limits.

I followed, fighting my conscience every step of the way. What was I doing?

*You don't know him, Jane.*

*Dear Self: Shut up. I'm trying not to be so safe and boring.*

I waited a moment and the pushed through the doors and plunged into the dimly lit room. Only one or two small bulbs hanging over the center of the room illuminated enough to show dark shadows and bookshelves. I wandered through, getting lost in the shadows and the stacks. That is, until I heard noises.

Laughter, soft erotic kind.

Gasps and groans, the sexy kind.

Oh God. I had followed him, captivated like a fool, and he was having some assignation. God, I sounded like a relic using words like *assignation.* Clearly I had been reading too many Regency romance novels. Jeez. Alas, I had intruded upon his illicit midnight rendezvous.

Except it wasn't illicit because this was the twenty-first century and this was what people did and it was OK. But I was interrupting his hook-up and that was *not* OK.

Thank God I had put this mask on. Thank God it was dark. Thank God my clothes were dark—charcoal grey pencil skirt and thin, black cashmere sweater set—so I could better blend in to the shadows. Thank God he didn't know me. All I had to do was just quietly slip out and forevermore remember why I was a girl who *didn't.*

I turned to go, taking a few steps before walking straight into a wall of books.

"Ow. Damn."

The couple paused in their sighs and moans. For just a moment, the sounds of a frantic kiss ceased.

There really ought to be better lighting in these facilities. For safety's sake. Just the right amount so a girl could make a discreet exit without injuring herself. Resolved to speak to the janitorial staff about it tomorrow, I inched along, tracing my fingers along the spines of books as a guide.

More laughter.

More heavy breathing.

The sounds of a kiss turning to something else.

I turned the corner at the end of the row of tall stacks. In the faint lighting I could just make out three aisles of shelves running perpendicular down the room. They were only waist high. The party people had littered the tops with empty beer bottles and half-drunk glasses of wine and champagne. Masks were strewn about, as well as stray sets of headphones with the thumping bass pumping through faintly.

Now was not the time to tidy up, however much I was struck by the inclination. *You're too neat, Jane. You're too "just so," Jane.*

"Shut up," I whispered to the voice of Sam in my head. I took a deep breath. There were only two ways out of this room. I could double back and attempt to navigate the darkest, farthest aisles—hopefully not encountering That Guy and his very loud girlfriend.

Or I could go directly toward the door. On my hands and knees so that I wouldn't be seen. I didn't know where the couple was in this cursed room. They could be anywhere.

I did not want to be seen. I didn't know That Guy and he definitely didn't know me. We ought to keep it that way. I certainly didn't want to meet him under these circumstances.

There was a shuffling noise. I held my breath, waiting. More sighs and more moans.

I dropped to my hands and knees and started crawling and I started praying that I'd get out of this room without being discovered in such a ridiculous position. Of all the things I'd been wishing for lately—Sam to want me back, a book deal, a pay raise, a new dress from J.Crew—getting out of here undiscovered was top of the list.

The sighs got louder. So did the murmurs and moans. Either this girl was a drama queen or That Guy Was. That. Good. For a moment, I paused, wondering what it would be like to completely disregard any sense of decency, respectability and get it on in a public place.

Once upon a time I'd had the chance. It had been during study hall, senior year. *C'mon Jane . . . Meet me in the stacks.* Sam had grinned, sliding his finger in through the belt loop on my skinny jeans, playfully trying to tug me along for an illicit rendezvous in the local public library. I had laughed nervously and pushed him away.

Tonight I wondered: What if I could ditch my unyielding sense of modesty and wrap my legs around a man as he took me up against a wall of books? What if I didn't bite back sighs, moans and cries from the touch of a man determined to bring me to the brink of outrageous pleasure?

I didn't do it back then. Instead I had told the love of my life, "*Shhh . . . We'll get in trouble.*"

I should have said yes. Because he never asked me again.

I definitely should not have shushed then—*or now.* I knew the rush of that shaming, condemning hiss had escaped my lips when that girl fell quiet.

"Hello? Who's there?" the girl asked from somewhere in the darkened room.

"It's nothing," a guy said, presumably the one she was hooking up with.

And then I heard another man's quiet laughter. It seemed that . . .

Oh God. Please God, no, no, no . . .

Still on my hands and knees I looked up. Breathing kind of stopped for a second. He towered above me. And he was that kind of good looking—all thoroughly disreputable with a disarming boyish grin.

He'd caught me on my hands and knees. And shushing people.

"Need a hand?" he asked.

"I just dropped something," I said, frantic for an excuse. I blurted out the first thing that came to mind. "My mask. I dropped my mask."

"The one you're wearing?" The corner of his mouth quirked up into a sexy grin and I wanted to die.

I smiled in a please-kill-me-now kind of way and struggled to go from hands and knees to standing with some semblance of grace, while wearing a pencil skirt. The guy just watched with a cool, detached and bemused expression.

The sighs and moans carried on. Clearly it wasn't That Guy, since he stood before me. Alone.

"I know they're loud," he murmured leaning on the stacks and blocking my exit. "But did you really just shush them?"

I just sighed and gave him an annoyed glance, which hopefully communicated that this was a mortifying encounter that I'd rather not prolong.

"Let me guess. You're a librarian," he said with a hint of humor in his voice. "I mean, who else shushes people in a library? And a party."

"Actually, I am," I said awkwardly.

He laughed, a low rich sound without any mockery, just mirth. Laughing in the library was also something that usually elicited a *shhh* but I bit that one back.

"Are you going to kick them out for making out in the stacks?"

There was no need to clarify which *them* he was referring to. They were making their presence known. Loudly.

"No. I'm really sorry to interrupt. I didn't mean to. I'll just let you . . . finish whatever it is you were doing in here."

"Just had to take a phone call. Thought it would be quieter in here," he said, shrugging. "You're really a librarian?"

Yes. Who cares? I should be going.

He leaned against the stacks as if settling for a long chat. My heart started thudding and I wasn't sure if it was desire, anticipation or because this was the sort of situation that ended badly and on the cover of the *New York Post.*

"So what's your name, Sweater Set?" He asked, as he pulled out his iPhone.

"Jane."

"Jane what?"

"Sparks. Why do you care?"

*Jane Sparks, Age 28, hopelessly single and tragically flummoxed by attentions of hot guy at the library.*

"I'm looking you up to see if you're really a librarian. And if I should mention you in my tweet about getting shushed at the Hush party."

"Is that really necessary?"

They were projecting tweets about the party (#Hush-Party) on the large screens set up around the room. The last thing I needed was the whole party full of cool people—and the whole freaking Internet—knowing about this increasingly disastrous situation. I was the square who had just shushed people at a party. I had just interrupted a hot hook-up in the stacks. And I was trying to pretend none of it had just happened.

This was like high school all over again.

I didn't mean to. It wasn't like I was on some moral crusade. If anything, I was *trying* to be the exact opposite. But old habits died hard.

"There you are. Found you on Facebook," he said to his phone. "Jane Sparks. Librarian at the New York Public Library. So you weren't kidding."

"I just shushed you at a party," I replied. "Do I seem like kind of girl who has a sense of humor?"

"You seem like the kind of girl who needs a good orgasm."

"Do lines like that really work for you?"

"Not with the good girls," he said, and I didn't know what he meant by that. Good, as in well behaved? Good, as in actually dateable women?

"I'm Duke, by the way." He held out his hand and, always polite, I extended mine and we shook hands.

"That's a much better pick-up attempt," I said and then, catching how presumptuous that sounded, I added, all flustered, "If that's even what you're trying to do. Anyway. I'm really sorry for interrupting you."

"You're cute," he said, and I blushed in spite of myself. "I've never fantasized about getting a girl out of her sweater set before," he said, indulging in a long, heated gaze at my sweater set. In my defense, I had come from work. "But they say there's a first time for everything."

"Stop with the romantic compliments. I might swoon."

Duke laughed.

"I'll catch you, Sweater Set."

"I don't doubt that. What happens next is what I'm concerned about it."

"Mouth to mouth resuscitation," he said gravely. "To save you."

"I'm no damsel in distress," I told him. But I was. I was a mess. Heartbroken and finding my way in a strange city, still dreaming of the life that had slipped through my fingers when I wasn't looking.

"And I'm no hero," he murmured. He didn't look like one, that's for sure. He wore jeans, sneakers and a T-shirt that said, "Kozmo.com." Whatever that was.

Maybe I didn't need a hero.

Maybe I needed what happened next.

His hand slid around my waist, resting on my lower back.

His head dipped toward mine. Instinctively I tipped my face up to his.

Then it happened. His mouth on mine. Tentative at first, becoming all the more bold as I melted into it, much to my shock. But the more I tasted him, the more he demanded and the more I surrendered and forgot all my rules about first dates or at least knowing last names.

*I was the kind of girl who didn't do this.* But I was trying not to be that girl, hence the mask, hence the champagne that had gone straight to my head, hence this kiss. I threaded my fingers through his hair and dared to kiss him hard.

His hands spanning my waist. His hands, skimming higher. My breath catching in my throat. He, whoever he was, pressed me against the stacks. The hard edges of the shelves dug into my back. It hurt, slightly, in an oddly pleasurable way. I couldn't close my eyes and imagine I was anywhere else. No, there was no forgetting that Good Girl Jane was hooking up with a stranger. In public.

Jane didn't.

*Oh yes she did.*

"Take this off," he whispered urgently, tugging at my cardigan. In our frantic and tangled efforts, we ended up knocking over a swath of all those champagne glasses and bottles of beer. They clinked together, shattered, fell to the floor, making a delicious racket.

I had no thoughts of stopping to clean them up.

*You don't even know him!* My brain shouted. But I just arched my back, let my head fall back and sighed with the pleasure of it all.

I could feel him, hard, pressing against me and I wanted him desperately. Didn't know his last name. Didn't know anything about him. Didn't even care. I heard more sighs, more moans and I vaguely realized they were mine.

I ran my fingers through his soft hair. The stubble on his jaw was rough against my neck as he pressed hot kisses and gentle bites on my skin. I gasped in shock not just that he did that, but that I liked it.

I felt something vibrate against me and for a second I thought all my dreams had come true. But I realized it was just his phone in his pocket.

He pulled back, easing me down to me feet. I found my knees were weak.

"Sorry, Sweater Set, but I have to take this," he murmured before kissing me and disappearing into the shadows.

## *Chapter Two*

*Bar Veloce—the next day*

*@TechCrunch: Duke Austen's startup, Project-TK, is rumored to be seeking $150m investment at a $1.2 billion valuation. Here's why it might not happen:*

Is the third time a charm for Silicon Alley party boy Duke Austen? After the spectacular flame-outs of his first two startups, he's on the verge of a major win—as long as investors can overlook his reputation for hard-partying and worries about him paying more attention to the hot supermodels instead of hot new products. Even if he gets the funds, Austen's prospects of remaining in charge of the company he founded are slim, unless he cleans up his act. Read More . . .

"This." I set down the damned invitation on the bar.

"What is *this*?" Roxanna asked, looking up from her iPhone. We often met here after work for drinks and supper before returning to our microscopic, claustrophobia-inducing Chelsea apartment.

"*This* is the invitation to my tenth annual high school reunion. In other words, I have just been invited to a party to showcase what an utter failure I am."

"What are you talking about? You have ditched Bumble-fuck, Pennsylvania, and your boring ex-boyfriend for the glamorous life of a single working girl in New York City."

"I'm working as a library assistant, which is a step down from my previous job as head Librarian. I told everyone I was going to write a novel but I only have a word document that reads 'Untitled Romance Novel' and not much else. And I still love my ex-boyfriend, thank you very much. And he's been dating. I saw it on Facebook. I have *not* been dating."

"No, you're just having hot and heavy hook-ups with strangers. Much better if you ask me," Roxanna said with a grin. I had told her a little bit about what had happened at the party last night, leaving out the most embarrassing bits. Which is to say, I left out most of the story.

"*One* hook-up. Once. And while I was pawing at some random guy in the library like an adolescent, everyone else has gotten married and had children. Look—" I said, pulling up the list of my friends on Facebook, many of them from Milford High School. "Melissa, married. Has a baby. Rachel and Dan, married. *Two* children when some people don't have any! Kate Abbott, who was totally horrible to me throughout high school is 'seeing someone special.' And it's only a matter of time before Sam posts MARRIED! BABY! He keeps posting about dinners at all romantic places around town."

"What, all three of them? You have to unsubscribe to his status updates," Roxanna said dryly.

"I don't know how," I grumbled. "Technology mystifies me."

"Here, let me see if I can do this on your phone," Roxanna said. I handed it over without a second thought. "I'll take care of this while you pine away for the days of card catalogues, horses and bayonets."

"We were voted Most Likely to Live Happily Ever After," I said glumly.

"Aww, should we go home and look through your yearbooks?" Roxanna asked, pushing her red hair over her shoulder.

She was tough as nails and just what I needed. In return, since she was a disaster at things like laundry, cooking, and paying bills, I helped make sure she had clean clothes, Wi-Fi, and didn't subsist exclusively on bourbon and popcorn.

"No, it will only make me feel worse," I said with a sigh. I knew because I had already looked through them. It was all the inscriptions that slayed me. *Stay in touch. Don't ever change.*

Growing up, I had this idea of what my life would be like, and I did everything I could to make it happen. Good grades, good school, career in the library sciences, which would allow me some flexibility when Sam and I married and had kids.

We planned to get engaged after he finished his dissertation. Then he'd get a job as a professor at the nearby Montclair University.

We planned to have a house on Brook Street—I knew just the one—with great bookshelves and a yard for the kids. Maybe a couch from Pottery Barn.

Then POOF—fired. Then POOF—dumped.

Sam had coldly explained that he wanted to see more of the world. Date other people. Be with someone more adventurous. Someone who didn't have every detail of her life already pre-ordered.

"Ah, this will make you feel better," Roxanna said when the bartender set down our drinks: a glass of chardonnay for me and bourbon on the rocks for her. "Cheers."

"I just had this idea of what my life would be like by now," I said as Roxanna messed around with my phone. "And so did everyone else. I had already planned my wedding on Pinterest. Now he's squiring some girl around town to all the romantic spots while I'm working at the low level job I had in college and I'm hopelessly single."

"Personally, I wouldn't give a fuck what my loser high school classmates thought of me," Roxanna said, sipping her bourbon and still messing around with my phone.

"I know. I'm seething with jealously."

Truly, I kind of was.

"But since you clearly do care, why don't you show up with a totally hot, successful date?"

I sighed and smiled. "It would make everyone jealous, wouldn't it? No one would ask me if I missed my old job, why Sam and I broke up or how my novel writing is going. The problem is your plan requires me knowing a hot, successful guy. The only guy to ask me out since I moved here is José at the bodega."

"Speaking of hot, successful guys, *why do you have a friend request from DUKE AUSTEN?*" Roxanna looked up at me, her blue eyes wide and her mouth open in shock.

"Hey, why do you still have my phone?"

"Jane! Is this the guy you hooked up with?" Roxanna held out my phone showing the Facebook profile of That Guy. All dark eyes, tousled hair, unshaven. Like a pirate or a highwayman or some rogue up to no good. Yeah, that was the guy.

"I think so. It was dark. I had a mask on," I said. I figured he was just some charming but scruffy guy who was probably a struggling actor who tended bar at some hipster dive in Williamsburg. Totally un-dateable.

"OMG," Roxanna said. Gasped, really. "OMG."

"What?"

"Jane, this is DUKE AUSTEN," she practically shrieked. Then she looked around as if someone might overhear this conversation. As if he were Somebody.

"I can see that. But who is he?"

"He's only the billionaire co-founder of Project-TK. See, you do know someone hot and successful. OMG do you ever!"

"He didn't look like a billionaire."

"Why? Cos he didn't wear a suit and grey tie and wave

around fat cigars and a bottle of 26-year Macallan? Welcome to the startup world, Jane. Where the billionaires look and act like the guys next door."

OMG, indeed.

"He caught me on my hands and knees," I whispered, horrified. "And shushing people at a party."

"And then he hooked up with you. I spent all day working on a story about him, in fact," Roxanna said. She grinned wickedly before launching into everything I needed to know about him. "His company is seeking a series C-round of financing but everyone is freaking out because he's a brilliant disaster and they're afraid he'll blow it like he did in his first two companies. Even if he gets the money, the investors might force him to step down. He can code and he can sell anyone on anything. But then he was always getting wasted and missing work or getting embroiled in all sorts of scandals with models. And there are rumors of drug use. He's all kinds of bad news."

"Why can't I just find a nice guy with a steady job and benefits?"

"Oh, the romance. Oh, be still my beating heart," Roxanna said dryly. "I have an idea."

Roxanna grinned wickedly and started doing something on my phone. I reached for it, and she lunged away. "Hey, Jane, watch the drinks."

"Roxanna, what are you doing?"

"This."

She held out the phone.

Heartbeat: stopped.

Breathing: stopped.
My life: Over.

***Duke Austen was tagged in Jane Sparks' life event***
*Jane Sparks and Duke Austen got engaged*

Everyone would see it. My mom, my dad, my sister. Everyone from Milford, my co-workers at the library, everyone I had ever known that had an Internet connection. Sam. He would see it.

And then all those people would see that it had been a joke, a prank or the desperate and wishful thinking of a lonely girl. Haven't I had enough mortification?

I couldn't do it again. I couldn't answer all those people saying sweetly (or not so sweetly) "I thought you were with so-and-so. What happened?" It hurt too much to always say *I don't know* when things kept going wrong.

Instead, I shrieked and lunged for the phone knocking over my class of chardonnay. It shattered, spilling all over the bar and dripped down into my nude patent pumps. My life was in shambles. And there was wine in my shoe.

"What have you done?" I gasped.

"I just got you a hot date for your high school reunion. You're welcome."

"No, you just got me a fiancé!"

"Even better, right? I hope he gets you a giant diamond ring," Roxanna said dreamily. "Although, he's probably only a billionaire on paper—or he will be once

Project-TK has their IPO. But don't worry, I'm sure he's got a few actual millions tucked away."

"How do I undo this?" I frantically jabbed at the screen. It was so unsatisfying.

"I have no idea," she said with a shrug. "Facebook settings are impossible to figure out."

"Roxanna!"

My phone dinged with an incoming text message from a number I didn't recognize.

***917-123-4567:*** Meet me at Soho House in ten minutes for celebratory drinks.

***Jane Sparks:*** Who is this?

***917-123-4567:*** Your fiancé

## *Chapter Three*

*Soho House, the roof—twenty minutes later*

```
if (pretendFiancé === "Jane" ||
fauxmance === true){
console.log ("There is hope for me yet.");}
else {
console.log ("I'm screwed. Again.");}
```

"HELLO, SWEATER SET." The infamous Duke Austen leaned against the bar and murmured the words with one of those devastating smiles that were most often found in the pages of romance novels.

This smile, however, was real. In spite of my best intentions, it made my heart skip a beat.

"My name is Jane," I corrected, as befitting someone who was in fact wearing a dove grey sweater set. They were comfortable, classy and part of my work wardrobe.

I looked totally overdressed next to him, in his broken in jeans, sneakers and a T-shirt that said "Friendster."

Duke didn't reply—he was checking his iPhone and ordering himself a bottle of Becks and a chardonnay for me. I sat there thinking it was ridiculous we were even meeting. This could have been dealt with over email. Or the phone. Or Facebook, if I could figure out how to delicately and kindly break up with someone over that technological marvel.

But I couldn't, and it seemed that breaking up with one's faux fiancé ought to be done face-to-face. I hadn't consulted Emily Post, but I was sure she would agree. And I had to ask him what the hell he meant by celebratory drinks.

Also, he asked me to meet him at Soho House, which had a fabulous rooftop bar and was members only. This was likely my one chance to go.

"So," he said, leaning against. "How've you been?"

"Since last night? Worse and worse. You?"

"Better and better. Especially now that you're here."

"You sound like you plan to continue this engagement. You know that it was a stupid prank by my friend? I didn't actually mean it. We are not actually engaged. We hardly even know each other."

"We'll get to know each other, Sweater Set," he said in one of those low, shiver-down-the-spine kinds of voices, and I knew exactly how he'd earned his bad reputation. The murmurs. The gaze. The devastating smile. It was appalling.

I couldn't make this stuff up.

"I was hoping we could break off this 'engagement,'" I said. "If we changed the settings now and I posted a status update to the effect of 'Haha, drunk friends!' I could play this off as a prank and everything will be fine, though I already have *eight* missed calls from my mother. I thought maybe you could help me with the damned Facebook settings. I've heard you are knowledgeable about this sort of thing."

If he was some brilliant tech guy, I figured he could help a girl update her Facebook privacy settings and undo the most disastrous status update ever.

"Why would I want to do that?"

"Because—" Then I stopped, flummoxed. "Why wouldn't you?"

Duke leaned in real close. That grin again. The one that made me think of clichés about butterflies and racing pulses . . . and rakes and rogues and a slow, torturous seduction. In my defense, I'll say that really, you had to see this man *lean*. You had to see his smile and the dimple in his left cheek and the flexing muscles of his forearms.

I hadn't noticed these things last night in the dark. But oh, did I ever notice them now.

My mouth went dry. I took a sip of wine and thought about how I hadn't had any physical affection since Sam and I had broken up months ago. Well, other than last night. And to think, I'd never expected to see this guy again. He was supposed to be my one time wild fling. And he was here, murmuring my name.

"Janet."

"Jane," I said with an exasperated sigh.

"I didn't have to accept it," he said. "I didn't have to share it, either."

"You did what?" I gasped. He ignored me.

"I didn't have to ask you to meet me here. Do you want to know why I did?"

"Because you have a warped and twisted idea of fun?"

"True, but no. Your prank—"

"My friend's prank."

"—has possibly solved a major problem for me."

"I'm so glad," I said dryly.

"Hear me out. One drink. Out of the kindness of your heart. You seem like the kind of girl who does things out of the kindness of your heart."

"Fine," I sighed. Because I was. Because it was a gorgeous early summer night on the roof of Soho House and maybe I'd see a celebrity.

"Project-TK is growing fast but to get big enough to IPO we need to raise another round of funding first. If we can go public, a lot of people stand to make a shit ton of money, myself included. But investors are nervous about me and it's negatively affecting our ability to raise funds at the valuation I want. I seem to have earned a reputation for—"

"For drinking, possible drug use, excessive partying, and orgies with models. And for generally being unreliable. A 'brilliant disaster' my friend said."

"You're informed," he said dryly.

"My friend works for Jezebel.com."

"That explains so much," he said.

"So no one wants to give you money because you

have demonstrated that you're completely unreliable . . ." I prompted. If nothing else, I could glean some good gossip, break the engagement and sell the whole story to Roxanna for a month's rent.

"This is big, like Google or Facebook. Or it could be. I've got two major fails behind me and I can't let it happen a third time. Do you know why they really call me the bad boy billionaire? Because I made and *lost* a billion bucks. Project-TK is a chance to redeem myself. I have to raise the money and make sure the investors don't get ideas about forcing me to step down. Isn't there something or someone you would do anything for?"

"Maybe." Yes, but he didn't want me to. Damn you, Sam.

"I would do anything," Duke said softly, and he was earnest as hell now. His eyes darkened as he looked at me. "And what says mature and responsible like marriage? Especially to a goody-two-shoes like you."

"What makes you think I'm such a good girl?"

"To start, you were shushing people at a party."

"That was just one little thing."

"You're right. What about what happened *after* you shushed me?"

"A one-time lapse in judgment," I said stiffly. "I'm not that kind of girl."

"Well, for me it was just another Tuesday."

I gasped.

"Exactly. I need you, Janine," he said with pleading expression. "Just for one weekend."

The words that should have come out of my mouth: "No" or "You belong in a mental institution" or "Go to hell" or "MY NAME IS JANE GET IT RIGHT." Instead, I opened my mouth and what came out but a question.

"One weekend?"

"A bunch of us are flying out to the valley to meet with potential investors and bankers about the deal. It had been made clear to me that if I'm not on my best behavior, I'm out. As I said, I've got two major busts behind me and I'll be damned if it happens again."

I wanted to ask what happened. But it seemed bad. Like, doesn't talk about it bad. Like, I was better off Googling it later.

"If you're such a brilliant, billionaire tech entrepreneur, what do you need investors for?" I asked. I wasn't an expert in math, but something wasn't adding up.

"I cashed out of my first startup before it went bust and I'm set for life, but I don't have enough to take Project-TK to the next level. But I will be a billionaire if I can pull this off." He paused for a moment. Then he added, in a low voice, "It's not about the money. It means that much to me. I can't be the guy that always chokes."

His passion was clear and for a moment, it left me speechless. His eyes had darkened and he spoke intensely. I couldn't help but wonder what it would feel like to be wanted with the intensity that Duke wanted success.

"Third time's a charm, right?" I murmured. It was all I could think of to say.

"C'mon Janine. It'll be an all-expenses paid weekend in San Francisco for you," he said, a faint grin and playful touch of my hip.

"One weekend in which I pretend to be your plus one."

"Just for a few dinners, cocktail hours, that sort of thing. I'll be in meetings with a bunch of stuffy, boring bankers and lawyers, bored to death and playing games on my iPhone while pretending to answer emails. You can shop, schedule spa appointments, work on your novel or whatever. As long as you behave, and even more importantly, make sure I do."

"My novel? How did you know about that?"

"I'm assuming you have aspirations to write one, given your Facebook status updates about moving to the city to write a novel. Or maybe you can spend the weekend brushing up on the security features of your phone."

"I thought I could trust my friend. Apparently not over drinks," I muttered.

"Drunk girls are the worst," he said with a grin. "In the best way."

"If I had a ring, I would hand it back after a comment like that," I replied. "Honestly, whatever happened to acting like a gentleman?"

"This is going to work perfectly. You're so prim and proper."

"I haven't agreed yet."

Duke just smiled and my temperature started to rise. It was just a *nice* smile. There was temptation and promises and mischief and I caught myself holding my breath for what came next. That smile, it was a prelude and lord help me, I wanted to know what this man had in mind.

That is, until it happened.

Duke dropped to one knee. He clasped my hands in

his. A hush fell over the rooftop. All the fabulous people suddenly were interested in me. Us. This farce.

"Jane, will you marry me?"

I looked around—everyone was watching this scene unfold. A few even had their camera phones held aloft in spite of the waiters telling them no cameras were allowed. This video would be on YouTube within minutes. If I said no . . .

It'd be one more awkward thing to explain to everyone. His investors or whatever would think he was crazy. I'd surely never see him again. I'd return to my regularly scheduled life of shelving books instead of hot and heavy hook-ups against the bookshelves.

If I said yes . . .

It'd be an adventure. I wouldn't be *Jane who didn't* or *jilted Jane* or *just Jane.* I'd be Jane who moved to Manhattan and snared the bad boy billionaire. People did not give *her* the pity eyes.

But then again, the whole thing was a total lie and eventually the charade would end with another break-up. Then I would definitely get the pity-eyes from everyone. *Poor girl pretended to date a guy. How lame!* I couldn't do it.

Duke squeezed my hand.

My lips parted but no sound came out.

He stood, beaming, and kissed me full on the mouth.

"She said yes!" he declared, even though I had done no such thing! The bar erupted in applause. The manager brought over bottle of Veuve Cliquot on ice.

"What the hell was that?" I hissed.

"Smile, darling," he said, handing me a glass of champagne. "They're still watching."

I smiled. Oh, did I smile. But inside I was in an advanced state of shock. Did he really just do that?! What the hell just happened?! Stop giving me that smile and stupid smoldering glance!

"You owe me," I said. "You owe me big time. You owe me so much I doubt even you can afford it."

"Name your price, Sweater Set," he said, clinking our champagne flutes together.

"Besides remembering my name?"

"You can ask for more than that," he said softly.

He couldn't give me the one thing I wanted: Sam. I still held out hope that he was just going through a phase and would eventually realize what we had—and could have. Then we could get back together and buy that house and live happily ever after.

And if that was too much to ask . . . I sipped my champagne and puzzled it over.

I wanted to feel *good* again. Successful, loved. Not a hot mess one step away from complete disaster. I wanted to be like my old self: Jane who had her life totally together.

And if *that* was too much to ask? Then I wanted everyone to *think* I totally had my life perfectly together. I could write the novel, like I'd said I would. But Roxanna was right. I needed a totally hot and successful date for the reunion.

"I need you to be my date for my high school reunion."

"That's it?" he asked, pleasantly surprised. As if he expected me to ask for a few million bucks.

"Yes. I know, it's ridiculous but . . ."

"No, I get it," he said quietly. "I was the voted most likely to end up in jail, as well as most likely to win the Nobel Prize."

"How did you manage that?"

"It had something to do with the FBI arresting me at 14 for hacking the *New York Times* to make the front page headline about blow jobs preventing cancer. Still couldn't get me a date to prom, though. They obviously don't keep abreast of the news. What about you, Janie? Most popular?"

"Hardly. I spent too much time in the library studying. Most Popular was Kate Abbott, and her favorite extracurricular activity was making my life miserable. However, I was voted least likely to be arrested."

Over a glass of champagne we smiled and for the first time I thought we're maybe not so different after all. We were still trying to prove ourselves to people who never cared about us in the first place.

"C'mon, Sweater Set," he said taking my hand in his. "We have to go hack a love story."

## *Chapter Four*

*Duke Austen's Penthouse Apartment*

```
var jane = { name: "Jane Sparks", age: 28,
looks: "hot" }
```

WE HOPPED IN a cab and Duke told the driver to take us to the corner of Bowery and Bond. The car lurched into traffic immediately, heading east and speeding through the tree-lined streets of the West Village.

"Where are we going?"

"My place."

"I think that's moving a bit fast, fake relationship or not." And then, when he didn't answer because his head was looking down, riveted to his glowing iPhone screen, I asked, "Who are you texting?"

"My dev team. I'll explain later. Why don't you text

your roommate where you're going. Tell her if you're not home by tomorrow morning—"

"—to call the police and that you're the number one suspect. Already on it."

*Jane Sparks:* Hey, off to Duke's place. We're going to hack a love story (wtf?). Call the cops if I'm not home in a few hours.

*Roxanna Lane:* K. And congrats on your engagement!!!!!!!!!!!!!!!!!!!!!!!!!!

I clicked on the link she sent. It took me to a YouTube video of Duke on bended knee before me. Behind me, the Manhattan skyline lit up against a dusky purple sunset sky. There were 347 views. Already.

*Jane Sparks:* OMG that was just fifteen minutes ago!

"The video of our proposal is already online," I told Duke.

"I know," he said, still typing like a madman.

I took a moment to check Facebook out of habit. 46 people had already liked our "engaged" status. I started to read the comments until I read one the said, "Wow congrats! Didn't even know you were dating someone!" Ugh.

My mom called *again* and I ignored it.

*Roxanna Lane:* Um, also I got a tip about the story. Can hold off for an hour or two if you want to prep but then I've got to go post something or lose my job. Xo!

"So you know my roommate, the gossip columnist?"

"Mmmm."

"People are already talking about us. She says she had to publish a story on it ASAP but she'll give us an hour or two to prep, whatever that means."

"Already on it."

Duke put his phone in his front pocket.

The cab slammed to a stop. Horns blared. Pedestrians swarmed around the car, like a rushing river around boulders. He turned to face me.

"Jane . . . You can still get out of this. You can get out now and walk home and we'll laugh this off as a practical joke and then pretend it never happened."

"Or?"

"If you come home with me, there's no going back. No pretending it didn't happen. We're gonna make this real."

I had made it this far . . . From the quiet, sleepy streets of Milford to the always loud, always bright streets of New York City. Sam's kiss was no the longer the last one on my lips. I'd already overcome *Jane Who Didn't* a little bit, more and more. It started with a kiss, a drink, a prank, this cab ride and could lead to whatever the night held. I was scared of all the unknowns. But I knew I couldn't go back to being the Jane who was fired and jilted and spent the past six months in quiet and lonely desperation. Something had to change.

"Let's go," I whispered.

The cab lurched forward and made a sharp right turn, launching me right into Duke's lap. He caught me and didn't let go. In the dark back seat of the cab with the city flying outside the windows, he kissed me. Pulled me onto his lap, tightened his arms around me, and kissed me.

I kissed him back, even though I wondered if this was part of the ruse or if it was something else. I kissed him because I was lonely and because his kiss chased away the cold I'd been feeling these past few months. His hands were warm, caressing the bare skin of my back. I felt him hard beneath me. I hoped we were stuck in traffic. For a while. Because when he kissed me, I forgot everything.

We broke apart only when the taxi came to a stop in front of a modern building on the corner of Bowery and Bond.

THE ELEVATOR DOORS closed behind us and after one hot, frantic kiss with me pressed against the walls the doors opened to the penthouse, revealing a large, modern space. I was sort of breathless from the kiss, but still had to gasp at his apartment.

One wall was purely glass, showing a breathtaking view of the uptown Manhattan skyline including the Empire State building and the Chrysler building. The living area opened to a large kitchen and dining area decorated with stainless steel appliances, granite countertops and top-of-the-line fixtures. The long dining table was covered with massive, wafer-thin Apple monitors.

Two guys and two girls stood around the kitchen

island, sipping bottles of Miller Highlife and working on sleek Mac laptops.

They looked up when we arrived.

"Jane, meet my dev team. Rupert, Kyle, Amy and Jessica. This is Jane. My fake fiancé."

Rupert spit out his beer. The others burst out laughing. I glanced up at Duke; he was clearly enjoying this.

"Hi," I said awkwardly. "Nice to meet you all."

"Congratulations?" Jessica asked.

"We saw the video. Nice proposal, dude," Kyle said. He and Rupert wore faded T-shirts under open plaid flannel shirts with broken in jeans and sneakers.

"Thanks. It's only a matter of time before the rest of the world sees it and starts Googling us. In fact, I know it's started already," Duke said. "So if we're going to pull off this whole 'I'm engaged to Sweater Set and settling down' thing, we need a backstory that goes back further than last night when Jane and I met."

"Go on."

"There's no proof of our relationship online, other than that video. So we have to create it. The problem is that Jane here is still living in the nineteenth century, technology-wise."

I opened my mouth to protest. It's not like I used an AOL account and still had dial up.

"So we need tweets, check-ins, stupid lovey-dovey pictures on Instagram," Amy said.

"Exactly," Duke said.

"A sex tape. You should totally make and leak a sex tape," Rupert suggested with a lecherous chuckle.

Jessica, Amy and I rolled our eyes.

"Jane?" Duke questioned.

"That is not happening. At all. Ever."

"Exactly the reaction I was expecting. A second option, which will be slightly less fun, is hacking Twitter, Foursquare, Facebook and Instagram to create proof of our longstanding, secret relationship."

Ok, he had me at *secret romance*. This was the kind of thing I loved reading about in paperback novels after a long day. It was the kind of story I'd considered writing one day. Or maybe I'd start tonight? *A Secret Romance* by Jane Sparks. In fact . . .

"Like the movie *Green Card*," I said, smiling at the thought of one of my all-time favorite romantic comedies.

"I haven't seen that one," Kyle said.

"What?!" I might have gasped in shock. Then I remembered that he was a dude and I was a chick and thus the same movies we did not watch.

"That's because you were six when it came out, dude. In 1990," Duke replied.

"Gawd, Duke, you are old."

"Shut up, infant."

"I think they used a Polaroid camera to take pictures of themselves," I ventured.

"What's a Polaroid?" Rupert asked, smirking.

Duke tossed an empty beer can at his head proving that he at least didn't act much older than these guys.

"I just Googled it," Kyle said, peering up from his laptop. "Google says it's a kind of vintage camera equipment."

Duke reached for another beer, presumably to throw at Kyle and quite possibly to hit and explode over what appeared to be thousands of dollars of computer equipment that we apparently needed to use desperately. Tonight.

I touched Duke's arm, the slight pressure enough to remind him to restrain himself. He looked down at me and whispered, "See? I need you."

"Where do we begin?" I asked.

"Kyle, Jessica, and Amy are experts in Python, Scala and C, so they'll hack into Twitter, Foursquare and Facebook and create past check-ins, tweets, and all that. Rupert is a genius with Photoshop. Basically these guys will create the "proof" of our relationship that anyone would find if they searched for us. Which they will do, if they aren't already."

"I'm going to pretend I understand what you just said," I said, and Duke grinned. "Can you really make all that stuff happen?"

"Sure," Duke said easily, as if I'd asked him if he could breathe. "Python, Scala and C are programming languages. We just need to get into the system and write the story we want to tell."

"I'm sure we can manage it, given enough beer," Rupert said.

"And blow jobs," Kyle added. The lady coders and I rolled our eyes.

Duke threw a full beer can at him, and that time I didn't try to stop him.

"You can see why we need a romance novelist," Duke said.

"Obviously these guys are clueless about that stuff," Jessica added with a withering glare.

This was an excellent point. I was the resident expert in romance—especially of the fictional variety. Sam used to laugh at me for reading those "trashy" novels. I couldn't even imagine how he'd react when he found out I was writing one. But I'd worry about that later.

For the moment, I just wanted to revel in the feeling of being wanted, needed, and considered good at something. It'd been a while since I'd felt that way.

"Hey, Jane, what's your Twitter info?" Amy asked.

"I'm not on Twitter," I replied, and there were exaggerated gasps all around.

"Well you are now," Amy replied with a grin. "Your handle is now @Jane_Sparks."

"What about Foursquare? Instagram? Facebook?" Jessica asked.

"I'm on Facebook."

"Ok, let's start setting up accounts for her," Duke said.

"What's your password?" Amy asked.

"I'm not giving you my password!"

"Janet, they're about to hack into some of the biggest sites on the web," Duke said. "They can work around your password but it will save everyone a bunch of hassle if you just tell us now."

"Sam0924," I confessed. If I had known I'd be sharing it, I'd have changed it to something less embarrassing.

"Who is Sam?" Duke asked.

"Her dog. Everyone uses their dog's name for their password," Amy said.

"My ex-boyfriend, actually," I explained, blushing. "And the date of our first kiss. I just haven't gotten around to changing it. I've been busy." Yeah, real busy moping, feeling sorry for myself and day dreaming all the possible scenarios in which Sam will decide he wants me back.

"When did you break up?" Duke asked.

"Six months ago."

"Which means we started going out, say, five months ago," he said. "That gives you a month to get over him. That's enough, right?"

I burst laughing.

Over Sam in one month?! Over the love of my freaking life in just thirty days?! I'd spent the past six months in damp, grey haze that left me cold and unable to see out. In a fit of despair I had left the only life I'd known and moved to the city and threw myself upon the mercy of my college roommate. I did nothing but work and miss him. Every amazing thing I saw in the city, I wanted to tell Sam about it. After every hard day, I wanted nothing more than to curl up in his arms and whine about it to him. I hadn't just lost my boyfriend but my other half.

You don't just get over that kind of loss in *a month.*

Besides I believed in the *Sex and the City* girl math that you had half the total time that you were together to get over a guy. That is, until I took this moment to actually do that math. Six years. I had six years to get over him. I had six years to wander around, miserable, missing him.

"Oh dear God," I muttered under my breath. These

past six months had beaten me down. Now that I thought about it, I wasn't sure I'd survive another six months. Let alone six years.

"What is it?" Duke asked, glancing over at me.

"Nothing," I said. It had to be nothing. I could try to win him back. But I could not just sulk and pout and *wait* for him anymore.

"OK, Sweater Set, let's get started creating our faux-mance. What was our first date? Make me look really good."

And so it began. I created a series of perfect dates and romantic moments. Duke's developers made it all "real" through backdated tweets, check-ins, status updates and pictures.

As the hours ticked by that night, Duke and I created an entire relationship. Our first date was dinner at a cool restaurant on the Lower East Side, followed by drinks at on the Soho House roof. We went out for after work drinks at Tom and Jerry's, took long rambling walks in Central Park on Sunday afternoons, romantic dinners at downtown restaurants and evenings at parties. Anyone who really knew me would know it was out of character of me to hook up with a new guy so quickly and stay out so late, so much. Hopefully they'd believe that a whirlwind romance with the hot bad boy billionaire had changed me. The most important thing was that Duke's investors believed that he'd met a Nice Girl and settled down.

"How are those tweets coming, Jane?"

"Working on them," I said hurriedly. Having never tweeted before, I was slow at crafting the perfect, 140 character description of romantic dates with a guy I hardly knew.

***Drinks with my guy @DukeAusten at Angel's Share.***
***Sunset in central park with @DukeAusten. pic.twitter.com/W4iRVWwbCT***

"Good, because I'm in Twitter," Jessica said. "Your spoof email worked, Duke. Some moron clicked through and entered their email and password. From that I was able to get in and reset the admin password."

"We need some pictures so I can Photoshop the shit out of them," Rupert said, grabbing his iPhone.

"Won't it look suspicious if all our pictures are taken at night?" Duke asked.

"And in the same outfits?" I asked.

"Isn't there an Instagram filter to fix that?" Jessica asked.

"There will be by the time I'm done tonight," Amy said.

While Kyle, Amy, and Jessica worked on their hacking, Rupert, Duke and I grabbed a bottle of champagne and headed out to the terrace to take some photos.

"Smile kids! You're engaged!" Rupert said, starting to snap pictures of Duke with his arms around me. The two of us smiling shyly at each other. The two of us laughing at this absurd situation. The two of us toasting and drinking with celebratory glasses of champagne.

And then a funny thing happened. I wanted to blame

it entirely on the champagne, but I couldn't. I started to get swept up in the moment. All the sparkling city lights, all the bubbly, all the laughter and kisses and the feeling of us keeping a secret from the world . . .

We clinked our glasses together. CLICK! My heartbeat quickened.

We each took a sip. FLASH! It went straight to my head and I felt dizzy.

We smiled because we had a secret. FLASH! I thought about kissing him.

I smiled like Duke was my one and only true love and I was thrilled at the prospect of a lifetime together with this man. It was the smile I used to give when I saw Sam. When Duke smiled like I was a woman he'd love, adore and worship forever, I started to feel warmth spreading from my belly.

It was the Champagne . . .

It was the way he looked at me. It was the way it felt real.

But how could this scruffy guy in a T-shirt and jeans, this brilliant disaster, fall for me, the bookish girl in the sweater set, knee length skirts and pumps that shhh-ed him at a party? It was absurd. This whole scheme was absurd. But it was too late to back out now.

The only thing to do was not screw it up and make sure I didn't fall for him. I had to remember that this was just an epic practical joke. It wasn't real.

"Um, maybe you guys should kiss or something."

Duke set his glass down and cupped my face in his hands. His eyes searched mine: was he asking for permission? Forgiveness? I didn't know, I didn't care. I lowered my lashes and tilted up, heart beating fast as I awaited his lips upon mine.

FLASH!

His mouth was firm, I yielded. My heart, it pounded. Duke ran his fingers through my hair, gently cradling my head. *Hold still, don't go.* As if I'd want to. As if I could. The memory of Sam's kiss was fading and I was too intoxicated to reach out and hold onto it. I clung to Duke instead.

FLASH!

"Um, OK. I think I got enough pictures of you two kissing," Rupert said awkwardly. "I mean, one is enough and I got more than that. Glad you guys are so thorough. The internet will thank you."

"Let's get a few more inside," Duke said. So we took a bunch more where we pretended to be on a tropical vacation, at a crowded rock concert, or on a sunset sail on the Hudson.

"We should do a few of us on the couch," I suggested. "You know, for all of our romantic nights in, just the two of us."

"Good idea. But those should be selfies," Rupert said. "It'd be weird otherwise. I'm going to head back to the kitchen and get started on Photoshop.

"Oh! Can you put in me in cute outfits?"

"Not sure what that entails but I'll try," Rupert said, laughing.

"Anything from J. Crew," I told him.

"Sweater sets!" Duke hollered after him.

We crashed on the couch and Duke pulled me close, arm around my shoulders.

He held out the camera and we took the goofy, silly pictures you take when you're in love and always laughing and fooling around and just enjoying each other's company.

I caught myself laughing too hard, leaning in too close, pressing a kiss on his jaw and breathing him in. *It's not real Jane.*

I was brought back to reality by a text message.

***Duke Austen:*** Enjoyed meeting you last night. Let's do that again sometime.

I glanced up at him. Was this real? Or part of the story? There was laughter in his brown eyes. I decided to play along.

***Jane Sparks:*** A pleasure. Let's definitely do it again.
***Duke Austen:*** Are you free tonight?

I laughed because he was right next to me. Really close right next to me. I was all too aware of him.

***Jane Sparks:*** I'm kind of in the middle of something.
***Duke Austen:*** Working on your novel?
***Jane Sparks:*** Some kind of love story ☺

Research. Yes, research. That's what this was. Because if I was going to write about bad-ass rogues who could make a good girl break the rules with just a kiss, I probably ought to spend some time with one.

"Jane," he whispered.

I turned and lifted my gaze to his. Our mouths met for another kiss, as if we were helplessly drawn together. My lips parted, his too. The kiss deepened. A rush of breath. A surge of heat. The pounding of my heart and the desperate urge for more, more, more.

"Dude—" Kyle called out. "We're stuck trying to access Twitter's database. They must have been drunk when they coded this."

They hacked and coded and did whatever on the computer until late, late, late at night or crazy early in the morning. They chugged Red Bull and beer. I sipped Champagne and wrote gushing tweets, posted Facebook statuses, and approved Photoshopped outfits I could never afford in real life. Sometime around three in the morning I fell asleep on the couch. The last thing I remembered was Duke draping a blanket over me, dimming the lights and kissing me goodnight.

## *Chapter Five*

*Word count: 3,765*
*Jane's twitter followers: 48*
*Boyfriends: 1 (fake)*
*Jobs: 1*

*258 West 15th Street, Jane and Roxanna's apartment*

ROXANNA KNOCKED ON my bedroom door, leaned against the doorframe and gazed at my tiny room. The twin bed (all that would fit) was covered in clothes and an open suitcase. My laptop was open to *Untitled Regency Romance*, to which I had added the words "by Jane Sparks."

Even better, I had added words. Thousands of words. A story was starting to take shape. Wallflower (me) meets the dashing Blake Auden, Duke of Ashbrooke (aka Duke Austen). Fake engagement ensues via the Regency version of Facebook, otherwise known as the newspaper.

Oh, and there were meddling friends of course. It felt so good to finally be writing. I'd always thought about it and occasionally mentioned it, but Sam had just laughed. Everyone had just laughed.

"I can't believe you're doing this," Roxanna said with a grin as she watched me carefully fold and pack sweaters. "It's so unlike you. I freaking love it."

"It's totally crazy. I have officially lost my mind," I agreed. I still couldn't quite believe I agreed to any of this—the fake engagement and the weekend away in San Francisco that I was packing for.

Roxanna ambled over to my dresser and rummaged through. She pulled out a pair of pink lace underwear and tossed it into my suitcase.

"And I'm not packing that."

"Why not?"

"Because he's not going to see my underwear. This is a strictly business arrangement. It's *pretend.*"

Even though those kisses didn't feel fake and even though pretending made my heart skip a beat. The last thing I needed was more heartache. So I just had to keep my heart out of it.

"You never know . . ."

"The whole point is that I am a total good girl. And good girls do not . . . Hey! What are you doing?"

But it was obvious: Roxanna rummaged through her Marc Jacobs handbag and pulled out a handful of condoms. She dropped them like confetti into my suitcase.

"Safety first!" Roxanna said cheerfully.

I just gave her A Look and a weary sigh because I couldn't argue with her.

"You know you want to," she said. My only response to *that* was to tuck the condoms discreetly into a side pocket.

"Was he not a good kisser?"

"He was good." There was no lying about that.

"Was he clumsy?"

"No. Not at all." There was no lying about that either.

"And you don't want to sleep with him?"

"I didn't say that." Because I did want to. I hadn't felt lust—just lust—in a while. Sam had been my one and only and we'd been together for just shy of twelve years. If I slept with Duke—or whoever else—it would be truly saying goodbye to the life I had lived and the life I had planned on. I didn't know if I was ready. And I didn't know how explain any of that. "It's just more complicated."

"Um, no it's not, Jane. You see, when a boy and a girl are reasonably attractive and they drink alcohol . . ."

"I think maybe I could fall for this guy. I mean, I don't know how to separate sex and feelings. And if I fall for him but he doesn't like me then I'll be dumped *again*, only this time, not just everyone in Milford will know. The whole Internet will know! There's nowhere to run after that."

"Oh, Jane. You take everything way too seriously and you're way too overdramatic about it," Roxanna said. "I say that with love. As a friend."

"It turns out I might have a mind for fiction after all."

"Are you writing all this down?" She asked with a nod toward my open laptop.

"Every word," I said, grinning.

"What if he reads it?"

"I'm writing a historical romance novel. I'm not great at math, but I think odds are in favor of Duke not reading it. At all. Ever."

"Famous last words," she said with a laugh. "But really, Jane . . . this is a once in a lifetime opportunity for all sorts of fun. Don't let it go to waste, OK?"

Later that night—after a few more hours agonizing over just the right outfits that suggested demure, abide-by-the-rules girl—I had finished packing. Included in my suitcase: sexy underwear and plenty of condoms. Just in case.

Roxanna was right: I took everything way too seriously. *If* I did start falling for Duke, I could just channel those feelings into my writing, which would free up my heart and conscience to have some well-deserved fun with the bad boy billionaire.

## Chapter Six

*Word count: 5,321*
*Jane's twitter followers: 483*
*Boyfriends: 1 (fake)*
*Thoughts of Sam: 34*

OUR ENGAGEMENT MADE headlines on TechCrunch, Gawker, ValleyWag, SiliconAlley Insider, and Betabeat. The morning after that, we got a mention on Page Six of the *New York Post*. The day after that I boarded a flight to San Francisco with Duke. Virgin America. First class.

The flight attendants fawned over him. *Do you need a blanket? A glass of champagne? A magazine? Anything?!* Duke took this flight regularly (JFK→ SFO), so they all knew him. I wondered just how well . . .

After I refused Duke's offer to join the Mile High Club, he popped a pill and washed it down with a glass of champagne.

"What are you doing?" I asked, appalled. I was supposed to make sure he wasn't up to his usual boozy, drug-addled antics. And it was only nine in the morning.

"Relax, it's just a sleeping pill."

I accepted a complimentary glass of champagne and pulled out my laptop, determined to write.

"What is that antique you're lugging around?"

"It's a laptop computer. Maybe it's not the latest model, but it's not like it's a typewriter or anything." I'd also been kind of broke lately but didn't want to say that to the multi-millionaire beside me.

Duke pulled out his phone and tweeted or texted or whatever. I opened the Word doc with my novel. *Untitled Regency Romance Novel* by Jane Sparks was no longer just a blank page. It was a story, and one I was determined to have written and published by the time my high school reunion rolled around in just under three months. As long as I was mining this real life "love" adventure, I would be fine.

I glanced at Duke. My inspiration.

He yawned, put on the eye mask and went to sleep. Shit. I would have to make stuff up.

I started to type, imagining everything that had happened in the past week as if it were happening in nineteenth-century London instead of twenty-first-century New York City.

*"It seems we are engaged," the Duke of Ashbrooke remarked casually. As if he were only commenting on the weather. As if they were acquainted, and not complete strangers to each other.*

*"We did nothing to dispel the rumors," Emma replied.*

*"Rumors? It was printed in the paper."*

*"Very well, libel," Emma corrected, yet again wondering who had sent the cursed—and false—engagement announcement to the newspaper. "But you could still cry off."*

*She so kindly gave him the opportunity to live down to her expectations. She found herself holding her breath and glancing up at his impossibly handsome profile.*

*"Do you not want to marry me?" he asked, as if that had anything to do with it. She had not even considered it.*

*"Your Grace, I don't even know you."*

*"A minor detail, and one that is easily remedied." Then he glanced down at her with dark eyes and a suggestive smile. "It would be a pleasure to become better acquainted."*

*He said this, of course, in a manner that left no doubt as to what sort of pleasure or acquaintance he intended.*

***Jane Sparks***

*10 minutes ago near San Francisco, CA*

*Romantic weekend with my new fiancé! —with Duke Austen.*

When we arrived at our hotel around lunch time, everyone from the check-in girls to the bellhops fawned over Duke. *Could they help him with anything? Did he need anything?* The girls, especially, checked him out. At first I had just seen a charismatic, but scruffy guy. But he was really good looking and he carried himself like he mattered, like nothing would stand in his way. That alone was incredibly sexy. I wondered, too, if they knew about the millions. These girls saw. And they wanted. He didn't exactly rebuff them, either, treating them to seductive smiles that made a girl's resolve just melt.

I coughed. "Ahem."

Duke grabbed my hand. Kissed me on the lips. The girls sighed and looked away.

"See? You're helping already, Sweater Set."

Our room was a spacious suite on the top floor, with a balcony and a stunning view of the city. There was a king-sized bed in the bedroom. In the sitting room, in addition to comfortable couches and chairs there was a desk with a sleek new MacBook Air, plugged in and almost ready to go.

"Give me your vintage computer," he said. "I have a lunch meeting to go to, but I want to get started transferring all your data."

"Is that for me? I can't accept that," I stammered. I had looked longingly at them in the store until I saw the prices.

"This iPhone, too. Jane, I can't date someone who uses outdated electronics. It's like you dating someone illiterate. It wouldn't work and it's not remotely believable."

"Thank you," I said genuinely, grateful for the gift and oddly warmed by the thought and effort he had put into our fake relationship. "Who is your meeting with?"

"My CFO, Ethan. My lawyer. And our possible investor, Augustus Grey. Maybe some guys from the banks, too."

"Is that what you're wearing?" I eyed him warily.

His outfit of jeans, sneakers and a threadbare Pets.com T-shirt didn't exactly declare TAKE ME SERIOUSLY and TRUST ME WITH YOUR MONEY.

"Yeah," he said, as if he'd heard this all before.

"Shouldn't you put on a tie? Or a button-down shirt at least?"

Duke made a face. I just shrugged. "Whatever. I thought you wanted to appear respectable . . ." With a scowl, he stalked over to his suitcase and pulled out a wrinkled button down shirt and put that on over his T-shirt, leaving it open.

"For you, Sweater Set," he said with a half smile. "But I don't own a tie."

"Really?"

"Really. I'm off. We have a dinner thing at eight tonight. I'll come back and pick you up. Stay out of trouble."

"Isn't that what I should say to you?"

*Later*

`$(".tie").remove();`

"Well don't you look pretty," Duke murmured when he arrived back at the room at quarter to eight.

"Just for you," I replied. "And for whomever we are trying to impress at dinner tonight." Duke had given me no indication of what to expect at this dinner—fancy? Casual? Big dinner party? Small, intimate gathering? Given our conversation this morning, I figured those fashion distinctions would be lost upon him so I wore a black shift dress, nude patent pumps, pearl stud earrings and a whisper-thin black cashmere cardigan. I spent an hour blowing out my hair.

"Oh, and I bought you something," I said. He looked up at me from his iPhone, intrigued. I handed him the long, flat box. "Just a little thing from the gift shop."

I had also gotten myself a something: a hefty princess cut engagement ring, made of the finest cubic zirconia Duke's money could buy.

"Oh, Jane," he said with a laugh when he opened the box and saw. "A tie?"

"You said you wanted to be respectable," I protested.

"Yeah, but startup guys don't wear ties."

I rolled my eyes. I bit back thoughts of how handsome Sam looked when he dressed up in a suit. I could still recall the scent of wool and starched shirt. For our fifth anniversary, I'd gotten him silver cufflinks in the shape of books.

"Actually, do you know what we use ties for?" Duke asked in a slow, sexy manner that sent a tremor racing along my spine.

"No, and I'm not sure I want to," I said. "We have to go to dinner."

"Oh, I think you do," he murmured, smiling and letting the grey silk fall through his hands. "C'mon here."

I had a clue from the wicked gleam in his eye.

"We have to go to dinner in ten minutes."

"We can be late."

"I think that kind of attitude is what got you in trouble in the first place."

"So what's a little more? Besides, I thought we agreed that you didn't get in enough trouble."

"I don't know how you get away with this kind of stuff," I remarked. But I was intrigued. Tempted.

"Me neither," he said with a laugh. "Close your eyes."

I did. Oh, I did. I felt the silk cover my eyes and I felt him tie it in a knot at the back of my head. The world turned black and there was nothing but a heightened awareness of Duke's nearness. I inhaled, breathing in the scent of him. I could feel the warmth of him oh so close. My nerves started waking up and wanting to feel his skin against mine.

Duke started with a kiss where my neck curved to my shoulder while he possessively held my waist and pulled me close. Kisses, higher, my lips parted, wanting, until finally his mouth crashed against mine.

His phone pinged. A tweet or text or whatever.

He ignored it and unzipped my dress, sliding his hands across the bare skin of my back. Would he take it off? Did I want him to? Yes. God, yes. His hands kept roaming, his touch kept in check by the dress, clinging haphazardly but still *on*. Even though he couldn't see it, I was totally glad I had taken Roxanna's advice and packed sexy underwear, just in case.

I reached out for him, fumbling and feeling the soft cotton of his T-shirt as I pushed it aside, needing to really feel him.

"I think I might tie you up later," he murmured.

"We'll see about that . . ." I whispered. And then I forgot about that when Duke's palm closed over my breast and I gasped. The things he did . . . Bunching up my dress, his hand slid up to between my thighs, finding exactly the right spot and teasing me like crazy with slow, deliberate circles.

I unbuttoned his jeans. He sucked in his breath.

His phone started to ring. We ignored it. We kissed. We got a bit carried away.

Whoever called left a voicemail and then called again. Duke only pulled me closer and kissed me harder. Both of us, breathless. Both of us in ridiculous states of not-quite-undress.

Now the phone in the room started to ring.

"Sounds like someone wants to talk to you," I whispered.

"I'm busy," he murmured. Oh, I knew.

But the spell was broken.

"And I'm supposed to be making you respectable. And just look at me!"

"Oh, I am," he replied with a lingering, heated glance that took in my wrinkled dress and messed up hair.

I tugged off the tie and tossed it to him. "Wear this tonight. It's your turn."

"If that's how you want to play it, Jane . . ."

## *Chapter Seven*

*Word count: 10,251*
*Twitter followers: 621*
*Thoughts of Sam: 7*
*Thoughts of silk tie* and . . . : 103

One hundred and fifty million dollars on the line. One hundred and fifty million dollars of investment could propel one of the fastest growing startups into one of the biggest companies ever created. As long as Duke didn't fuck it up as he had in the past.

As we took the elevator down to the hotel restaurant I smoothed out my dress and thought about the money. I had learned, thanks to some Googling, that almost all the other VC's had passed. It seemed the success of Project-TK was reliant on a successful monetization strategy of their huge user base. Success was also a little too reliant on Duke's brilliant coding and magnetic personality. Unfortunately, he was notoriously unreliable.

I was here to help Duke convince the renowned venture capitalist, Augustus Grey, to pony up one hundred and fifty million dollars *and* to make Duke retained control of his precious company.

I was *not* here to indulge in tie-me-up, make-me-late-for-dinner sex. Already, this farce was off to a bad start. We were late to dinner.

The elevator doors pinged and opened.

"What are you doing?" I asked. He was fixated on his phone again.

"I'm checking in," he replied.

"Should I do that?"

"Go for it."

"Oh, look we get extra points for checking in together!" I exclaimed. I had no idea what the points were for, but I had extra!

"Shhh," Duke said, rolling his eyes. "You're supposed to know that since you've been on Foursquare for months and we've checked in a million times together."

"Right," I said, adjusting my dress, my cardigan, my hair . . . oh God, my hair. My blow-out hadn't quite survived our make-out.

As we approached the restaurant, we were directed to a private room where a bunch of guys like Duke milled about, drinks in hand. Not one of them wore a tie.

"So this might not be the intimate deal-closing dinner I had expected," Duke murmured to me as we crossed the lobby to the restaurant. "It looks like we have competition. Grey loves nothing more than to pit people against each other."

"I'm a librarian. Not an actress."

"No, you're a writer. Tonight you just have to compose your lines on the fly."

I smiled as we strolled up to the legendary VC, Augustus Grey. He was a distinguished guy probably in his forties with greying hair. His eyes were his most striking feature: blue, keen, intelligent and sharp. They missed nothing, those eyes. Nervously, I reached for Duke's hand. I didn't think we'd be able to pull this off. Beside him stood a young, handsome man. Duke whispered that he was Ethan Parks, the CFO of Project-TK.

"Duke Austen deigns to grace us with his presence. I am so honored," Augustus said dryly. Not a good start.

"I fancied some extra spending money so I thought I'd drop by," Duke said and I gasped audibly. I glanced up and saw him grinning. Ethan smiled tightly.

"As impertinent as ever. How predictable. How dull," Augustus replied.

"My sincerest apologies," Duke said. "I forget we are all here for the amusement of an ornery old investor."

"You'll do well to remember it, Duke. I might be the only investor you've got," Augustus replied with a pointed look. I couldn't believe the way these two spoke to each other. No wonder Duke had the reputation he did. If Duke secured the funding, it would be because of some criteria and formula that I'd never discern—and not because of his manners or respect for authority.

And then, all eyes shifted to me.

"This is my fiancé, Jane Sparks." Duke smiled and pulled me close as he performed the introductions—August looked skeptical and Ethan devolved into a sudden coughing fit.

"I'm pleased to meet you, Mr. Grey," I said.

"Are you really?"

For a moment I was taken aback by his abruptness.

"Yes," I said smiling. "I'm also very nervous." That brought a reluctant smile to his face.

"I suppose he warned you about this dinner," Augustus said. "Lots business and tech talk. I hope you're not too bored."

"I'm sure it can't be any worse than a blind date," I replied nervously.

"Ah, but you're not dating any more. You've snared this . . . gentleman," Augustus said in a manner suggesting that he used the term "gentleman" loosely.

"He's alright," I said smiling, "But it wouldn't hurt if he cleaned up a bit."

I was rewarded with a faint smile and gruff nod of approval.

"While I am just delighted you two are getting so well, I think Jane would like to meet the other guests," Duke said, taking my hand in his.

"I can't imagine she would," Augustus said. "They're a giant lot of boorish fortune hunters."

Said batch of boorish fortune hunters had the decency to shift awkwardly, glance down at their drinks and seem dismayed by the pronouncement. But it was the truth:

funding from Augustus Grey could be the key to their success. Duke and I were no different.

Dinner was a disaster.

If only the dinner conversation consisted of business and tech talk. Boredom would have been welcomed. Instead, Augustus and the others had questions about Duke and me.

We all took seats around a long, sleek wooden table. Chandeliers with Edison bulbs hung overhead. Each place setting contained fine, handmade porcelain plates, silver cutlery and delicate glasses. The restaurant was homemade, rustic chic that served farm-to-table fare.

Duke and I found ourselves sitting on either side of Augustus. Was it a mark of favor—or was he suspicious about our engagement?

"Welcome to dinner," Augustus began, raising his glass. "I know you all are ruthlessly competing for funding. If you are at this table, it's because I think your startup has promise. But I'll probably only decide to fund one of your companies."

"What criteria are you looking for?" asked a youngish guy with thick, black-framed glasses.

"I choose the winner based on criteria I will not disclose." His reply was followed by the sound of disgruntled murmurs up and down the table. "It is non-negotiable," Augustus said firmly. "If you do not think this fair, take to Twitter and see if anyone cares. Remember that you are free to leave at any time. Nor was your presence here required. In fact some of your presences were not even requested," Augustus said with a pointed look at Duke, who adopted an expression of utter innocence and said, "Fortunately, we have corrected that appalling oversight."

My mouth dropped open. *We hadn't even been invited to this dinner?*

Across the table, Duke just winked at me.

"You're lucky you're charming, Duke," Augustus said dryly. "Otherwise I don't know how your fiancé abides you."

"She has the patience of a saint," Duke answered. "And she likes her chardonnay. A lot."

"It's the only way to tolerate him," I replied dryly, with a dark look across the table at my "fiancé."

But Augustus's lips quirked into an approving smile.

"Indeed," Augustus said "Fortunately you've enough sense to settle down with a woman of wit and intelligent, though I have to question her judgment if she's marrying you. Now what was I saying?"

"That we are all competitors for funding and you will decide based on top secret criteria. Any complaints can be addressed to Twitter," Duke summed up.

"Well done," Augustus said plainly. "All your boozing and drugs haven't fried your brain after all."

"Why don't you just declare him and his *fiancé* the winners and let us all go home?" one of the other startup guys asked, not quite able to disguise the anger in his voice.

"After everyone has traveled all this way?" Augustus asked. "Duke and his fiancé could still screw up.

"To building the future," Augustus said, raising his glass. Everyone else raised their glasses as well. I nervously plucked my glass of white wine, but aware of skeptical and accusatory eyes on me, my hand shook and I dropped the wine glass. It shattered.

Across the table, Duke gave me A Look I couldn't quite read. Dinner had only just begun and already I had screwed up.

After the appetizers had been cleared, disaster struck again. A guy named Jack asked what would have been considered a polite and innocuous question under any other circumstances.

"So how did you two meet?"

"The news that Duke was engaged was one hell of a surprise," added another guy—I think his name was Justin. "Never thought he'd be the marrying kind."

My smile tightened and my stomach started to ache.

I looked to Duke, hoping the alarm I felt wasn't apparent in my expression. We had made up some tweets about our first date, but we hadn't concocted a story—especially one that we could tell in the cute couple-finishes-each-other's-sentences kind of way.

I thought of our flight from NYC to SF. I wrote and he slept when we should have been getting this stuff straight.

Duke just lifted his brow. I know—I was the writer. The romance writer. I should come up with this on the spot. But my mind went blank.

Apparently, his did, too.

"It was really romantic," I said, buying a little more time. And then I blurted out the first thing I thought of: "We met in the gazebo in Central Park. During a rain storm."

Of course I said this at the same time Duke said, "We met at a party."

"I didn't know Duke was the kind to take long walks in the park," Jack remarked, apparently not having heard Duke, thank goodness.

"I was on my home from a party. Couldn't get a cab in the rain," Duke explained. This tested the imagination of no one. It was a good save. But I knew why everyone was questioning us and it wasn't to hear a happy little love story.

If Duke and I could be exposed as frauds, we wouldn't get the funding, which would up their odds of getting it. One hundred and fifty million dollars. I could not forget that.

There was also the fact that Duke and I were so different and were an unexpected pair: He was gorgeous, magnetic, and all kinds of trouble who was known to have a preference for tall, leggy, skinny blonde models. I was the librarian in a prim shift dress and pearls who had made him wear a tie. In what world did a guy like him and a girl like me meet, let alone fall in love and promise each other forever?

"After your chance encounter in Central Park, did you propose immediately, Duke, or did you tweet about it first?" Augustus asked dryly.

"Did you guys date at all?" Justin asked. "Was there a whole relationship that went unrecorded on social media?"

"Check the tweets. And the Facebook updates. And Instagram," Duke said, grinning. I knew he was thinking about the triumph of the hacking that night and that he'd anticipated these questions. "When a man knows he's found the woman for him, why should he wait?" Duke mused.

A romantic sentiment? My heart thudded at the thought.

Or evading the question?

Definitely the latter.

"And how are the wedding plans progressing? Did you set a date yet?" Augustus asked.

"We haven't set a date. But I have everything planned on Pinterest," I said, and everyone laughed. Then I reached for my wine glass and made sure to flash my giant, cubic zirconia engagement ring.

From there, the conversation finally turned to and business talk, most of which I could not follow, like UX, API's and metadata. But every once in a while, Duke would catch my eye for a smoldering gaze across the table that made me shift in my chair. I was thinking of what would happen after dinner.

One king-sized bed.

One grey silk tie.

One bad boy billionaire.

One girl who'd been too good for too long.

I'd never been great at math but even I could easily tell what that added up to. Roxanna was right. This was a once in a lifetime opportunity. I needed to have fun and not waste a moment.

Duke was twisting that grey silk tie around his wrists and giving me A Look. I shifted in my chair, crossing one leg over the other. I might have sipped my wine, which did nothing to cool the surge of heat as I thought about my turn to wear the tie.

*Later*

```
$(".janesDress").remove();
```

Duke started loosening the tie in the elevator. It was going to happen. Me, him, that tie. There was no pretending otherwise. Part of me was ready to rip off my dress and his T-shirt—to hell with the security cameras. The part of me that was all feeling and no thoughts. But I took a deep breath, willing my pulse to slow and my nerves to settle.

It was just sex. I'd done it before. A lot. But not in a while, and not ever with anyone other than Sam. And never with a tie or any other toy. And definitely not with a guy like Duke, who by all accounts, had a thing for models and the prettiest girls.

So pardon me if I was nervous like it was my first time.

The elevator doors opened. We walked through them, and strolled silently down the hall. Duke put his hand on my ass.

"Really?" I asked, meaning to sound sarcastic but actually sounding breathless.

"Really."

Duke unlocked the door, I stepped in behind him and it softly clicked shut behind us.

"Hey," he said softly.

"Hey," I whispered. My heart was pounding. God, I was *nervous.*

"Now where were we?" He asked with a wicked gleam in his eye.

He gently tied the silk around my eyes. It wasn't what I'd expected—I thought he'd bind my wrists and do all sorts of wicked things to me while I was helpless to resist. Then again, the night was still young.

He unzipped my dress, and it fell with a *whoosh* to the floor. Taking my hand he led me away from the door. With my eyes closed I was at his mercy. For all I knew he could be recording this or taking pictures or—

I felt his jeans pockets for his phone. It was there.

"Much as I would kill for pictures of you like this, I won't take any," he murmured.

"I would kill you."

"You know, Jane, you could ruin me with this secret of ours. Remember that."

I could, couldn't I? He might have been the billionaire, and I was getting a favor out of this. But in the meantime, vulnerable as I was in this moment, I was not powerless in this relationship. If that's what it was. *Stop overthinking things, Jane.*

"Take this ridiculous T-shirt off," I said.

He laughed and I reached out and felt that his shirt was gone. His skin was warm to my touch. Palms flat, I explored his chest, broad, flat and strong. He sucked in his breath as my fingers gently caressed his nipples.

He kissed my smile. Hot, possessive, rough. As if this was something that he'd been wanting for days. If I was being honest with myself, I'd been craving this since the moment I first set eyes upon him at the Hush party. So I melted into the kiss I had craved. I tried to memorize the taste, the sounds, the feelings as if I knew deep down this wouldn't last. But then his hands pushed down the strap of my bra and he expertly unhooked the clasp. I sighed, feeling free.

He took my breasts in his hands, big and strong and his mouth, hot and wicked. I gasped. I sighed. I moaned. I was like That Girl in the library, but louder. I thought I'd die from this alone.

I was already ready for him. But he still wore his damned jeans and now he was—

"Never thought I'd say this, but I wish I had another tie," he murmured as he firmly clasped my wrists behind my back and sank to his knees before me.

"Oh," I sighed. His mouth, there. Me, in some sort of heaven. I exhaled slowly and allowed myself to surrender to all the sensations rocketing through me.

"Oh God," I moaned as his tongue traced slow, lazy circles around and around and around while a heat inside me started to build. My knees started to feel weak. I needed to touch him, run my fingers through his hair, hold onto to something because I was slowly but surely slipping away into that sweet oblivion. The pressure was building. Heat rising. I was gasping for air and couldn't get enough.

He didn't stop, no. Hell no.

"Duke . . ." He just kept doing that thing with his tongue and I really couldn't stand or breathe for very much longer. I was hit with that crazy, just-about-bursting desire. He released my wrists. Then he did wicked things with his fingers, his mouth, me, there and I was gone . . .

I cried out, loudly. I sank to my knees. He caught me in his arms.

And that was just the beginning.

He removed the tie, threw it aside, lifted me up and tossed me onto the bed.

Throw down, as Roxanna would say. Sam did not have throw down. And that was the last I thought of Sam all night.

Duke stripped off his jeans and everything else before joining me on the bed, settling his weight on top of me. I felt him, hard, pressing up against me and I was ready, oh so ready. "Jane," he whispered as if to ask permission, as if to ask if I had any second thoughts. As if I could stop now.

"Yes." Dear God, yes. I needed this, and I needed it now. I was so wet, so ready. He reached over to the bedside table, pulled out a condom, ripped open the foil, and put it on. My heart was still racing. My desire only increased. I moaned as he slowly pushed himself inside me, making me feel full, complete and totally at his mercy. I closed my eyes. Then he began to move with long slow thrusts that left me intensely aware of every sensation . . .

His stubble, rough against my neck. His breath in my ear revealing how much he wanted this and how much going slow was killing him too. His hands, holding mine, pinning them to the bed. I fought back at that . . . I needed to touch him.

Desperate for more, I wrapped my arms around his

back so I could feel him deeper inside me. Deeper and deeper, harder and faster. His mouth crashed on mine for a fierce, urgent kiss. I couldn't think anymore, I couldn't breathe I couldn't do anything but feel that insane pressure intensifying until I just. Could. Not. Take it. Anymore. I cried out, oh so loud, he gave a shout and we collapsed, catching our breath.

And that was just the first time. That night.

## *Chapter Eight*

```
$(".feelingsForJane").hide();
```

THE NEXT MORNING we woke up in each other's arms. I nestled into the warmth, having missed this kind of intimacy. For all the ways of connecting these days, nothing beat skin to skin. Nothing like a kiss, nothing like him slowly entering me, nothing like not being sure what was real and what was still a dream. It wasn't long before I was crying out in pleasure and it wasn't much longer after that before he came, too.

While he got up to shower and check email, I stayed in bed.

"Order room service. Go shopping. Write your novel. Whatever you want," he said, kissing me quickly on his way out. "I'll be in meetings all day."

I ordered a pot of coffee, French toast with whipped cream and a side of crispy bacon. Then I started writing.

Maybe, just maybe, I could finish this story and make an honest woman of myself. I indulged in a fantasy of showing up at the reunion with a published novel, and Duke on my arm. I may have fled the wreckage of my life and all the curious bystanders, but I could return triumphant.

The plot of my novel was ripped from my real life. But it was a romance novel, so I could be pretty sure Duke would never read it. He'd never know about the hero, the Duke of Ashbrooke, who was based upon him, including that wicked grin, the way that he moved through a crowded room like he was Somebody and the whole world got out of his way until one too many scandals and one fake engagement announcement changed the game.

I switched from my word doc to Google. Some research was in order. Fingers hovering over the keys, I thought about typing in DUKE AUSTEN. Did I want to know? Of course I did. But did I want to know from the Internet or from the man himself?

I texted Roxanna.

***Jane Sparks:*** Is it wrong to Google Duke?
***Roxanna Lane:*** I can't believe you didn't already.

I typed in the letters of his name, one by one, and clicked search.

Results came instantly. Duke, on every social network. His website, which included links back to his bio on Project-TK's webpage and more links of how to connect with him. His Wikipedia page was much more forthcoming with the information I sought. Even more revealing were the profiles and interviews with him in *Vanity Fair, Fast Company, Forbes* and *Time.*

The headlines alone were revealing: **Third Time's A Charm? Can Silicon Alley's Resident Bad Boy Redeem himself?**

From Wikipedia:

> Duke Austen, American tech entrepreneur, was the founder of two notable, but unsuccessful startups. His first startup, Findr.com, failed after questions were raised about its legality and the company declared bankruptcy from its legal fees—but not before Austen made and lost a billion dollars, earning him the name "the bad boy billionaire." His second company, Friend.ly, was named "one to watch" by *Fast Company* but lost its users to rival startup Facebook at an unprecedented pace. The failure is attributed to many missed opportunities and alienating potential investors and business partners by Duke Austen's failure to attend meetings, adhere to deadlines or maintain cordial business relationships.

*Vanity Fair* covered his early years with a six-page article, complete with glossy photographs of Duke in his apartment with the Manhattan skyline lit up behind him and with a bevy of gorgeous, scantily clad models draped all over him.

> After his parents died tragically in a car accident (which Duke miraculously survived), he went to

live with his aunt, Ada, who was a professor of computer science at the local university. When the boy showed signs of a genius level intelligence—and a series of disciplinary problems—she taught him to code and gave him increasingly difficult projects in order to keep him out of trouble.

It worked. To a point.

From the *New York Times*:

We would like to apologize for a recent security breach that resulted in an offensive article being published on our website. The perpetrator, a juvenile, has been apprehended by the FBI and will be prosecuted to the fullest extent of the law.

There were then pages and pages of pictures, featuring everything from stylized photographs for glossy magazines to blurry shots taken by camera phones at parties. Nearly all of them with girls, models, actresses . . . The kind of Done Up girls that made mere mortals feel so very not quite.

I was *so* not his type.

Which was exactly the point of this fauxmance.

Which was something I really ought to keep reminding myself. I glanced down at the sparkling hunk of rock on my left ring finger.

*It's not real, Jane.*

*It doesn't mean anything, Jane.*

*Two words, Jane: Cubic Zirconia.*

With a troubled heart, I clicked away all the articles and images and returned to my novel more determined than ever to make a success of since it was clear that Duke and I had no real future.

I wrote for hours. When I needed a break, I flipped through the hotel TV offerings and watched *The Hunger Games*, which totally sparked my imagination and sent me back to my story.

My room service meals came and went. I took a break to shower and dressed in a pair of skinny jeans, my grey sweater set (which I actually needed since it was crazy cold in San Francisco even though it was summer), black patent leather ballet flats and, just to drive the point home, a pair of pearl stud earrings. I didn't bother doing my hair since, with any luck, it'd just end up a tousled mess. Again. Instead I wore it in a bun high atop my head. Prim spinster, indeed.

LATER THAT NIGHT we survived another dinner. When I wasn't completely mystified by their tech talk, we were dodging more questions about our wedding, our first date, and when we knew the other was The One.

"Sometimes you just know," I said, but I was thinking of Sam. I missed the comfort I felt with him, which was the opposite of uncertainty and tingly anticipation that I felt with Duke. When he looked at me across the table, I felt the fluttering of butterflies in my stomach. My skin tingled, as if in anticipation. *Cubic Zirconia*, Jane.

"Jane makes me a better man," Duke told everyone. It

was exactly what everyone wanted to hear. I smiled and blushed and felt warm and lovely from the compliment. *Cubic Zirconia,* Jane. *Cubic Zirconia.*

Duke held my hand as we exited the restaurant. Everyone was watching, so I decided it didn't mean anything.

In the elevator up to our room, he kissed me so passionately that there was no doubting what was happening next.

Behind us, the door to our room clicked softly in the latch.

No one made a move to turn the lights on.

Any thoughts of real or not real, diamonds or cubic zirconia, faded. The only thing that mattered was his skin against mine. His T-shirt and my sweater set hit the floor. It all came off, a trail of clothes strewn from the door to the bed.

His mouth doing wicked things to me, kissing me all over. Everywhere. My mouth doing wicked things to him. All over. Everywhere. Hands caressing and exploring . . . until that tie reappeared. Duke wound it around my wrists, binding them together and leaving me under his control.

I opened my mouth to protest. He silenced me with a kiss.

I struggled slightly against the silk. Duke laced his fingers with mine and pinned my hands to the mattress above my head. His gaze locked with mine. For a second, I found it impossible to breath.

"You're gonna like this, Jane," he murmured. I knew

he was right. I was just . . . nervous and excited and curious and a bit scared and . . . his mouth closed around the pink center of my breast and I just sighed, sinking into all the exquisite sensations.

His hands roamed over my bare skin. I wanted desperately to touch him back. He laughed softly as I writhed under his touch. I only smiled wickedly in response. Even in the dark, he saw. He paid attention to the kisses that made me moan and the caresses that made me sigh. He discovered just how to touch me to drive me crazy.

Duke's fingers started to work their magic. I felt the heat increasing and pressure building. I was wet and ready and desperate to feel him inside me. And I was loud about it.

"Shhh, you'll wake the neighbors," he murmured. For the first time, I didn't care because I didn't know the neighbors and I wouldn't ever have to see them.

"Who cares about them?" I panted. If I didn't come soon . . .

Duke reached over to the bedside table for a condom, ripped open the wrapper and put it on. And tortured me with his hands and mouth some more. With the pressure building, I couldn't take it. I fussed with the silk tie, managing to free my hands.

Finally I could touch him and I savored the solid warmth of his chest. I skimmed my fingernails down his back and pressed my palm against his lower back and urged him to me. I needed him. Now. I couldn't quite manage the words. But I could cry out when he entered me at a torturously slow pace.

I writhed beneath him. We found our rhythm. Then we lost it in a frantic rush of almost too much pleasure all at once. I couldn't tell where I ended and he began. I cried out, overwhelmed. He groaned then shouted my name as he came.

We lay in bed for a while after that, just catching our breath and waiting for racing hearts to return to normal. The room was dark—but light from the city shone through the window.

We climbed under the tangled mess of blankets.

Beside me, Duke laughed softly to himself.

"I can't decide if you're keeping me out of trouble. Or not." He turned his head toward me and I saw the slight grin on his mouth.

"What do you mean?"

"On one hand, I'm not out at clubs, with other girls. And drinking too much, and getting into fights that are filmed and posted online before heading home with said girls."

*Girls. Plural.* I decided to let that one go. He was just a guy after all.

"But then again we're not exactly chaste and proper," I said, turning to face him. He rolled over onto his side to face me.

"Chaste and proper?" he said with a laugh. I blushed, in the dark. "Am I in bed with Jane Sparks or Jane Austen?" he asked.

"Haha." I'd been writing all day in Regency-speak and I didn't exactly have my wits about me enough to filter out old-fashioned language.

"But we're engaged, so it's OK," he said softly.

"Do you think people really believe it?"

"Sure. They want to. There's enough evidence that it's easy to."

"Project-TK means a lot to you," I said. Of course I *knew* that. But what started out as a crazy scheme was now turning into something bigger. I was afraid it would become *real.* Or that I would fall for him. I couldn't forget that—

"Yeah. Everything," he murmured. Project-TK was everything to him. I was doing him a favor and getting something out of it myself—namely, orgasms, travel and a date to the reunion. He was getting so much more out of this.

"I Googled you today," I told him.

"Only today?"

"Call me old fashioned, but I had this idea that I would learn about you from you," I said. "So tell me something that's not on the Internet."

Duke's expression became serious. Thoughtful.

"I'm not really engaged," he said quietly. I laughed and rolled my eyes.

"I know that."

"You know my one secret," he said. But I got the sense that there were more and that he wasn't sharing anytime soon. Of course, I was desperate to know. But I knew pushing wouldn't work.

"I used to nag Sam to tell me stuff."

"Your ex?"

"Yeah," I said. They we lay in silence for a moment.

Side by side. He pushed a lock of hair away from my face. "Aren't you going to ask what I nagged him about?"

"I'm assuming you wanted to know all his deepest thoughts and feelings," Duke said. "And you wanted him to tell you you're pretty and perfect and all that."

"Am I that predictable?"

"You're a girl."

"Ugh," I said and rolled over on my back to stare up at the ceiling.

"Alright, so here's something I've been wondering," Duke said. "I owe you a favor. Anything you want, I could give you. For example, I could have—and would have—written you a check for ten million dollars. You'd be set for life. And yet you ask me to be your date to your high school reunion. What's that about?"

I laughed softly. "I really sold myself short there, didn't I?"

"It sounds like you care what people think of you. A lot."

"I suppose it's pathetic," I said. But I could still feel the pity-eyes I got from everyone back home. And I could still feel the sickening sensation of the floor falling out from under me when, after I'd lost my job, my boyfriend of *twelve years* broke up with me. Gone, in just a second.

But Duke didn't give me the pity-eyes.

"Nah, I think I get it," he said. "I don't need the money from Project-TK. As long as I can afford all the Mac products I want, I'm set. But after my first two companies going bust so publicly, I need this one to work. I don't want everyone to think of me as Almost Makes It Austen. Or whatever."

"You don't spend much on your wardrobe do you?" I teased, needing to lighten the moment. It was strange to think that maybe he and I weren't so different after all. Because if that was true—if we had a real connection—then I could totally fall for him. I could think we had a chance to be real.

"Free T-shirts," he said with a grin.

"Everyone thought Sam and I would get married. They thought I had it all figured out—the job, the guy, the matching sweater sets. I miss that. In the meantime, I'll just do what I can to make it look like I'm not a total disaster while I figure stuff out."

"Do you miss having all that or do you miss everyone thinking that of you?"

Wasn't he an observant one.

"Yes. Both. I don't know." He smiled and laughed softly at my scatter-brained answer. "Do you know why I moved to New York? A moment of peer-pressure induced panic. I just blurted out that I was moving to New York and writing a novel."

"So you moved to New York and started writing a novel. Obviously."

"It's the pity in their eyes that I can't stand," I confessed.

"It's the worst," the Duke said passionately. We laughed. "I got it all the time after my second startup failed. I wanted to punch the person. It was bad."

"You know why Sam broke up with me?" While we

were having a heart to heart, I figured I might as well go all the way.

"Nope. And I'm not guessing either," he said. Smart man.

"I was too good," I said. Then, with a wry smile I added, "Too chaste and proper."

"If only he could see you now," Duke murmured.

"Yeah. Exactly." In a five-star hotel bed with a hot guy whom I barely knew and with whom I'd done all sorts of naughty stuff. The kinds of things that Sam had hinted at doing . . . But Duke just took control and made it happen and made sure I enjoyed it too much to protest.

"Should we take a picture for Instagram?"

*Yes. Look at me now!*

"No," I said, listening to my better judgment. ". I can't have naked pictures of me out there! What will people at work say?"

"You shouldn't care so much about what other people think," Duke said.

"Haha, coming from you!" I said. Then, tracing my fingertips along his chest, I asked, "What if you didn't care so much either?"

"Then we wouldn't be here," he said softly. Gaze fixed on mine. His hand caressing my waist.

"Yet here we are," I whispered.

"Just you and me," he murmured.

*Cubic Zirconia. Cubic Zirconia. Cubic Zirconia.*

But it felt so real.

## Chapter Nine

*New York Public Library*

*Word count: 48,006*
*Calls from Duke: 0*
*Tweets from Duke: 0*
*Facebook messages of any kind from Duke: 0*
*Text messages from Duke: BIG. FAT. ZERO.*

A FEW DAYS later I was back at the library, shelving returned books and wondering if I had made the whole thing up. Much of the weekend was spent in a blur of writing (me) and meetings (him). But then there were the stolen interludes in the morning and afternoon when he snuck back to the room. We locked the door and . . . Oh, I got all hot and bothered just thinking about it.

And then the nights . . .

Nights in which very little sleeping was done. Nights in which I didn't think in sentences, including the phrase "in which" because I wasn't thinking at all. I was just feeling his mouth, everywhere. His hands, skimming up my legs, playfully slapping my bottom, caressing my breasts, stroking my back and torturing me in just the place where it felt So. Damn. Good. His weight, on top me. Except for when I straddled him or I was bent over the bed or . . .

God, I was making myself blush. At work. Just thinking about him.

In that post-sex haze glow we stayed up late, having those intimate, exhilarating, confessional conversations before making love again. We were high on the thrill of fooling the whole world. Every hour that passed that this crazy deception seemed to work made us bold. We shared a secret. And we were fooling ourselves. Or was that just me?

We flew back to New York and shared a cab into the city. I wanted to ask him what happened next. Where did we go from here? Had it stopped being just a hoax—had a little bit of this been real?

But I, lust addled and on my way to falling in love, just kissed him instead. All the way from JFK to West 15th Street.

"See you later, Sweater Set," he murmured.

I pulled him close for one last kiss, grabbing a handful of his WebVan T-shirt. I savored the taste of him, breathed him in. Duke ran his fingers through my hair, pulled me close, and didn't let me go even though the meter was running. This kiss was costing him, but it wasn't anything he couldn't afford.

But that was four days ago.

I was increasingly vexed. It wasn't just the crash after the crazy sex high. It was those stupid late night conversations when we talked. About our *feelings.* I tried to just have fun. I tried not to overthink it. But the craving for him was intense and relentless.

His silence was devastating. It felt like rejection.

*Cubic Zirconia, Jane. Don't forget.*

I was at work on Thursday when I had to shelve books in the rare books room where Duke and I had first hooked up. The place was pristine and you'd never know what sort of debauchery had occurred up against those shelves or on the floor . . .

Had I made it all up? No, that had been real.

I texted Roxanna.

***Jane Sparks:*** He STILL hasn't called.
***Roxanna Lane:*** Tech guys don't call.

Right. They could build the whole freaking Internet but couldn't dial a phone number. Which they didn't even have to do anymore, they just had to touch the screen, once, and let it ring. He could at least say, "Siri, call Jane." It had never been easier to call a girl and they didn't. Just didn't.

***Jane Sparks:*** Well he hasn't texted or twittered at me or whatever. What do you think that means?

***Roxanna Lane:*** I think it means he's slammed with work because he's trying to score that big investment which every company dreams of. Why don't you call him?

Because I wanted him to call me. Because I read and wrote novels where it was forbidden for unmarried ladies to call upon a man, especially a bachelor. Because I'm still old fashioned. Because I might have bought a copy of *The Rules* when it came out. Because all that aside, I wasn't sure what was happening and I wanted reassurance from him. I couldn't be bothered to explain all that in a text message, so I just texted "Ugh."

***Roxanna Lane:*** Drinks later?
***Jane Sparks:*** Totes!
***Roxanna Lane:*** What did I tell you about using words like totes, obvs or adorbs?
***Jane Sparks:*** LOLZ ;)
***Roxanna Lane:*** Argh!!!!

But I wasn't LOL-ing or anything because I was in the library where it was deadly quiet. I had to keep my phone on silent. I also kept it in the pocket of my cardigan so I could feel it vibrate if Duke decided to remember that we were pretend engaged and wanted to get together for more of the crazy hot sex we had. For real. My phone didn't ring. Or vibrate. There was no word from Duke.

When I was in high school, crushing on Sam, I had figured out his class schedule and would take bathroom breaks only as an excuse to pass by his classroom and catch a glimpse of him. It had taken me weeks to figure out that he was in chemistry during third period, had algebra just before lunch or AP United States History when I had study hall.

Thanks to FourSquare, I knew that Duke had checked into Central Park with 29 others for a few laps around the park on his bike before my first cup of coffee in the morning.

When I checked into work at the New York Public Library he checked into Soho House for breakfast meetings.

I saw him check in at the Project-TK's offices.

While I grabbed a quick lunch at the bodega around the corner, he checked into late lunches the Breslin with Augustus Grey, his lawyer and other startup executives. He checked into bars after work—around eight or nine at night, when I was already home on the couch watching terrible reality shows with Roxanna.

I knew where he was at almost any given moment. I knew who he was with. I knew what articles he was reading, what songs he was listening to on Spotify. I saw pictures of his meals he didn't share with me, or sunsets he witnessed without me. I knew who he was friends with.

But I didn't know why he didn't call (or text, or whatever). I didn't know what he was thinking about me or feeling about me.

It was so strange to know everything and nothing about him all at once.

If he were really a tech genius he'd solve *that* problem.

An app for boys to communicate their feelings to the girls they were sleeping with. Make it multiple choice, whatever. Something, I just wanted something.

I finally got something later that afternoon. A text. My relief was palpable.

***Duke Austen:*** Put on your sweater set. Funding announcement in the morning, party tomorrow night. I'll pick you up @ 8.

*Bar Veloce—later*

"This. What does *this* mean?" I asked Roxanna, holding out my phone for her to see the text from Duke.

"Here let me see," she said, reaching for my phone.

"Paws off! Read it with your eyes not your hands," I admonished. I also took care not to spill our drinks. I desperately needed mine tonight and my usual chardonnay might not cut it.

"I can't believe you're still mad about that," Roxanna scoffed.

"Oh, I'm not mad, just wiser."

"But still totally flummoxed by your bad boy billionaire boyfriend."

"Is this a date? Or just part of our fauxmance? The man is a mystery."

"No he's not. You just can't read the code."

"I know. Trust me, I know."

I knew I was making this into A Thing. I should have

known that I couldn't have sex without feelings getting involved. Untangling what was real and what was fake was an impossible knot. And all I had wanted was a date to a party three months from now. I just happen to have gotten the best sex of my life and I wanted more of it. My life, too, had finally taken a turn to something adventurous, and exhilarating. I couldn't go back now.

"Are you having kitten feelings, Jane? Are you falling for him?"

"I write romance novels, Roxanna. Of course I'm falling for him." Of course, because I had trained myself to look for happily-ever-after and I had developed oceans of patience and hope that the hero would eventually *realize* that he was being an obtuse ass, to use the Regency term. But my patience was starting to fray and I was aching for his touch. "I just don't want to fall anymore if he doesn't return my feelings. So what do I do about this?"

"Put on a sweater set and your big girl panties and go to the party. But wear that sweater set with an insanely short skirt and ridiculously high heels and make him want you."

## *Chapter Ten*

*Park Bar*

Uncaught SyntaxError: Unexpected token {

I BOUGHT A new dress. It was navy blue, a perfectly respectable color. The neckline was so high it brushed against my collarbone, where Duke had kissed me and shown me just how delicate and sensitive a spot it was. The sleeves covered my wrists, where a Regency rogue might have dared a kiss upon a respectable lady. The skirt was wickedly short. I paired it with towering high heels, which nearly led to my premature death as I tried to walk down the stairs.

Duke picked me up at eight, just like he said. He was leaning against his car—a black Tesla Model S, along with a driver—waiting for me and watching as I walked toward him. For his big night of triumph he wore his usual outfit, this time with a Project-TK T-shirt. He grinned and whistled when he saw me, which was totally juvenile but totally effective in making me blush and making me feel hot.

Trying to get in the back seat, in the miniskirt, while retaining my modesty was just not happening.

"Stop laughing," I protested. "And don't look!"

"I've already seen you, Jane," he murmured once I'd gotten in and shut the door.

"Congratulations, by the way."

"On seeing you naked?"

"No, on getting your funding."

"I couldn't have done it without you."

In the dark we smiled at each other. He took my hand in his, when I wanted his hands all over me. I needed to taste him, to feel him, to be utterly possessed by him. As if he could read my mind, he pulled me close and kissed me hard until the car rolled to a stop in front of Park Bar on Tenth Avenue.

*Cubic Zirconia, Jane.*

But after tonight . . . maybe, just maybe it could become something real. With the funding secured, he surely wasn't beholden to anyone any more. We didn't have to "break up." We could just see where things went . . .

Or so I hoped. Desperately.

We skipped the line and went straight into the party, hand in hand. It was a mob scene. Everyone was keen to talk to him and desperate to get near him. I was jostled by the crowd and pushed farther and farther away from him until our hands were forced apart. He was the man of the hour. He was crazy rich. More importantly, he'd broken the spell. After two epic disasters, success was his.

Taking a deep breath, I went over to the bar and got myself a glass of champagne. Every so often he caught my eye from across the crowded room. I saw an apologetic smile. I saw the way he tried to move closer to me. It was his night. I didn't want to be the demanding bitch fiancé. So I hovered and let him have his moment in the spotlight and imagined what it must be like to be him right now.

Hours later I was back by his side, on my third glass of champagne as he talked about how thrilled he was with his success, how hard it'd been, how far he'd come, his vision and plans for the future. I eyed their ties . . . I eyed Duke . . . I'd never before felt desire that burned so hot and burned so bright. For safety's sake I should back off, but I was drawn to the warmth, drawn to the light, drawn to danger.

My heart kept forgetting we'd made a bunch of this up and certain other parts of me didn't care so long as it kept happening.

But how did you fake those late night, confessional conversations? It couldn't be possible. I thought it meant we had a chance because we had really connected.

How could he look at me like that—like he was imagining me naked—and not mean it? And could he tell how badly I wanted to rip off his T-shirt and everything else?

How could I crave his scent, his touch, the taste of him so intensely and so constantly? I had been drugged, surely. How could I live with an addiction like that?

Somewhere along the line this stopped being just about a hot date for my reunion, and I didn't even really care about his billions. I cared only about the true connection of a real embrace, skin against skin, mouth to mouth, heartbeat to heartbeat.

Finally, we found ourselves alone, relatively speaking. We were in a dark corner, his back to the room, as if protecting me from the crowd and creating a cocoon for just the two of us. We kissed the kind of kiss that if anyone saw it, they would have no doubts about us. My heart beat hard. A girl could dare to dream.

It was then, of course, that *my* phone vibrated with a text message. I had no intention of looking at it now, not when I was finally alone with Duke and maybe, just maybe, I might just might figure out if someone along the lines this story had gone from make-believe to my actual love life.

"Did you get a text? You have to look."

"Some of us can ignore our phones," I said haughtily.

"Some of us can't. C'mon check."

"Fine," I said, laughing. That is, until I read it.

I glanced up at Duke, curiously looking down at me, and held out the phone so he could read it.

***Sam Chase:*** Hey Jane. I'm in the city for a teacher's conference. Ended up with some free time, want to meet for a drink tonight?

I couldn't take my eyes off Duke as he read the message. My heart was pounding, as if his expression would reveal a clue about his feelings for me. It struck me that the text I'd been waiting months for was now completely overshadowed by what my pretend fiancé may or may not have to say about it.

Duke knew what this meant for me. In our late night talks, I'd told him a little more about Sam—how we'd been together since high school and how I didn't quite know myself without him. What I hadn't gotten to tell Duke yet was that I wanted to know myself with *him*.

This stupid text and how I only cared about what Duke would say just proved that I'd moved on from Sam. For the first time in my life, I imagined a different happily ever after for myself. The question was, how would my bad boy billionaire respond to it?

More than anything I wanted him to say *Forget that guy, Janet. Stay with me.*

"You should go," Duke said.

"What?"

And by *what* I didn't mean: "Hey this music is loud I didn't hear you." By *what* I meant "I'm sorry, you just said the totally wrong thing and I'd like to give you a second chance out of the goodness of my heart because I'm the kind of girl who does stuff out of the goodness of her heart."

"You should go, Jane. I'm gonna be here for a while. Lots of people I have to talk to. It'll be boring for you."

"You mean, since you've convinced everyone that you're all respectable now you want to have fun," I said, trying to laugh it off. But I'm afraid the bitterness came through. I didn't want to wreck his big night, but I needed some kind of confirmation or assurance from him and I was getting exactly the opposite. "Now you want your good little fiancé to go home, get out of the way."

"What is this about?" He looked wounded. I felt awful. I felt, all at once, every minute of every hour of every day that he didn't text or call or anything after I had bared myself, body and soul, to him. "I thought you still wanted to get your ex back."

"We have that weekend and then I don't hear from you until you need a date . . ."

"Jane. You agreed to all of this," he said, pushing his fingers impatiently through his hair.

"You forced my hand," I pointed out. "And I there is a video on YouTube to prove it."

I started to feel like I was drowning. Like we were cruising along and all of a sudden our car careened off the road, into a river with the water swiftly rising to the roof. I was powerless to stop it.

"I gave you a chance to get out of it in the cab, remember? But you agreed. Look, we can make a clean break after tonight."

"Is that what you want?" I asked. Say no, say no. Say you want me. Tell me to stay.

"What I want is to enjoy having raised one hundred and fifty million dollars and getting my company on track for an IPO when everyone said all the odds were against me and that I never had a fucking chance. I want to celebrate with you, Jane. But if you want to go, I won't stop you."

I wanted him to stop me. I wanted him to say, *C'mon,*

*Janine, let's get out of here.* I wanted him to say he didn't know what had happened but this wasn't just a game anymore. But no, he said *I won't stop you.*

Why should he? He'd gotten what he wanted—one hundred and fifty million bucks and a chance to succeed where he had failed before—with a hook-up on the side. And there were hundreds of girls in this room who would sleep with him. He didn't need me anymore. If he wasn't going to stop me from heading off to meet another guy, then I had to understand that he didn't want me either.

"I'm going to go," I said as calmly as I could. Meanwhile I gained a new understanding of the words *dying inside.* "Congratulations, again. Have fun tonight. You deserve to celebrate."

I started to walk away. Call my name. Ask me to stay.

"Jane!"

I turned around, my heart thudding so hard I thought it would explode. He grinned, faintly and said, "See you later, Sweater Set."

)};//End part one

What's next for Jane and Duke?
Check out this preview of

*THE BAD BOY BILLIONAIRE'S GIRL GONE WILD,*

the next installment of their story
from Avon Impulse.

*An Excerpt from*

## THE BAD BOY BILLIONAIRE'S GIRL GONE WILD

*Minetta Tavern*
*New York City*

DUKE AND I slipped into one of the intimate red leather booths in the back. The restaurant was small, dimly lit and decorated in the style of an old-school steakhouse. Duke ordered a glass of Macallan 18 and I could tell I annoyed the waiter by ordering only water.

"So are you feeling faint?" Duke asked, apropos of nothing.

"What are you talking about?" That champagne and dancing from earlier had gone to my head, but I wasn't feeling faint.

"The Ashbrooke Effect," he explained. When I looked at him blankly, he explained: "As in the duke of Ashbrooke. As in the hero of your novel. I'm assuming he's based on me. Vain, I know. But tell me, Sweater Set, am I making you weak in the knees?"

"I'm sitting down," I replied, as I started to get his references to my novel. Oh dear God, he had obviously read my novel that was based on us. Suddenly, my knees did feel weak, even though I was sitting, because I had been counting on the fact that bad boy billionaires don't read romance novels. Of course, Duke had to be the exception to every rule.

"You look a bit flushed," Duke continued, and I could feel the blush of mortification flaming across my cheeks.

"I've been drinking," I said, and took another sip of water. Frantically, I tried to recall the things I wrote and—I closed my eyes and groaned as I remembered.

"Feeling breathless?"

"I've been dancing," I replied. But really, how was I supposed to breathe when this guy had read the novel about us—that I had poured my heart into?

"Is your heart pounding with anticipation? His voice was real low now because he had cuddled up next to me in the booth and wrapped his arm around my waist, pulling me even closer.

"Yes," I gasped. "Yes."

My heart was pounding, I was breathless, and a little bit dizzy.

"I'm surprised you read it," I said, taking another sip of water.

"I had to know what everyone was talking about," he replied. "And then I had to be able to converse intelligently about it with the author."

"I didn't think you'd read it," I muttered.

"So you never thought that I would find out that you described me as 'so handsome that he sucked all the attention in the room toward himself, as if he possessed his own personal force of gravity.'"

"No, of course not." Otherwise I wouldn't have published it.

"Or described yourself as a plain wallflower?"

"Nope. And this is embarrassing," I said.

"It's a good book, Jane," Duke said. "No matter what happens, know that. If it didn't—"

"If it didn't what?" My brain snapped to focus.

"It complicates things," Duke said reluctantly, shifting so he wasn't holding me so close anymore.

"Because of Augustus?" I remembered the articles I read about their big—and overlooked—product launch because everyone was talking about my book and the anger of the big and overlooked investor.

"Yes," Duke said grimly. "But not just him. "I'm a private person, Jane."

I couldn't help it—I burst out laughing.

"What's so funny about that?"

"You share everything about yourself online! You're in the papers, the blogs, on Twitter, Instagram, and all over social networks I've never even heard of!"

"Yeah, but notice I never tell them anything really personal or revelatory about me. It's all about Project-TK or the industry."

"It's true, isn't it? You don't tell anyone what you're thinking or feeling. No one really knows you, do they?

Even me." I remembered being so frustrated knowing which articles he'd read, or having seen pictures of meals he ate, but having no idea how he felt about me.

"I told you things, Jane, that I never told anyone else. And now I see them published for everyone to read and make assumptions," Duke said.

I glanced up at him. His expression was inscrutable, but I saw the tension in his jaw. He took a sip of his whiskey.

"Ashbrooke . . . he's just made up," I said. It wasn't a total lie. Ashbrooke was fictional. He was just inspired by Duke.

"And Sam or Bennett or whoever?" Duke turned to face me.

"Alright, so I used a bit from my personal life."

"Did I ruin your date the other night?"

My heart was pounding again as I whispered, "What if I said no?"

"Everyone thinks you're mine," he said. "And I'm starting to believe it too."

"You say that as if it's a bad thing," I said.

There was something he was keeping from me. I could tell. It was there in the way he refused to meet my gaze and instead took a long sip of his expensive whiskey. It was in the way I had a sudden tremor of fear. All teasing aside, the success of my fictional book was causing real problems with Duke and me.

"Duke . . ." I rested my hand on his arm and tried to soothe away the tension I felt there. "I just wanted to write. I had something to prove to myself and to everyone. You understand that. I know you do."

He gruffly agreed.

"I could unpublish it, I guess." As soon as the words were out of my mouth, I regretted them. Because I could do it didn't mean I wanted to diminish my accomplishment in order to celebrate his.

"No, I would never ask that of you," Duke said strongly. "It's just that Grey is pissed that all the media attention was focused on my fiancé's "smutty bodice ripper"—his words not mine—

instead of our new product launch."

I looked into his eyes and there was no denying the truth.

"He's not the only one pissed," I said softly. "You are too."

Duke set down the now empty glass of whiskey hard on the table making the cutlery clink and the candle flicker.

"I just worked so damned hard to build it. It was a huge risk and everyone was skeptical, but I believed and I made my team believe, too. And now . . . for what? People aren't talking about it, which means they're not using it, which means I'm not able to monetize it, which means my IPO is in jeopardy."

"I'm so sorry." I was. I positively ached with remorse. I just never thought anyone would actually read my book, let alone people in the tech industry. "If it weren't for that blogger overhearing Roxanna talk about it, this wouldn't be an issue. I didn't plan this. I wouldn't ever plan this. I am so sorry."

"It complicates things. The reason we're together is so

that your good girl image can make me seem like an upstanding, responsible guy. And now you wrote this book that has everyone thinking we're a sham. And then there are pictures of you dancing on a banquette."

"What?" I gasped. He grinned wryly and handed me his iPhone. The picture was dark, but light and clear enough: I was standing on a banquette with Roxanna beside me; we were both singing along to the song, waving our arms, and sipping our glasses of champagne.

"That was from two hours ago!"

"I don't want to do this, Jane but—" There was a tense moment of silence when the waiter arrived with another glass of Macallan, which Duke immediately sipped from.

"You're going to pick your company over me," I said flatly. Why, why, why did my heart ache to say the words? I knew from the start that things between us were just pretend. Except somewhere along the line, my feelings for him became all too real.

He gazed down at me, blue eyes full of sadness. That was what started to undo me—he did care. But I had fucked things up.

The champagne buzz was starting to wear off and a headache was taking its place.

"I want you both," he said softly. "But things can't go on like this. I can't ask you to give up your work for mine. But I can't slack off on Project-TK now. We're prepping for the IPO, Jane. 20 billion dollars are on the line here. This is bigger than me and you."

"I get it," I murmured. And then, gazing into his eyes, I confessed: "I just don't like it."

This was the closest we'd come to talking about our feelings. What remained unspoken, but was finally understood, was that this was no longer just an act for either of us.

I could see it in his eyes. This guy liked me. Wanted me. Was tortured because of it. I could also see that his brilliant, billion dollar brain was coming up with an alternative course of action.

"Or . . ." he murmured, eyes lighting up. "We put the word out that we've broken up."

Telling people we had broken up wasn't the same as actually breaking up.

"Just thinking as a novelist here and not a jilted pretend girlfriend—do you think a break up right now will really quiet all the rumors that we faked a relationship so you could score a one hundred and fifty million dollar investment?"

"You wouldn't be a jilted girlfriend. We could still see each other in secret."

"A secret romance," I murmured. "I'm the one who's supposed to come up with that stuff."

"Fodder for your next book," he said with a grinned. "What do you say, Jane? Want to be my secret lover?"

This was the closest we'd come to talking about our feelings. What remained unspoken, but was finally understood, was that this was no longer just an act for either of us.

I could see it in his eyes. This guy liked me. Wanted me. Was tortured because of it. I could also see that his brilliant, billion dollar brain was coming up with an alternative course of action.

"Or . . ." he murmured, eyes lighting up. "We put the word out that we've broken up."

Telling people we had broken up wasn't the same as actually breaking up.

"Just thinking as a novelist here and not a pitied pretend girlfriend—do you think a breakup right now will really quiet all the rumors that we faked a relationship so you could score a one hundred and fifty million dollar investment?"

"You wouldn't be a fake girlfriend. We could still see each other in secret."

"A secret romance," I murmured. "I'm the one who's supposed to come up with that stuff."

"Fodder for your next book," he said with a grin. "What do you say, Jane? Want to be my secret lover?"

**Continue reading for a sneak peek of**

***THE WICKED WALLFLOWER,***

**the historical romance Jane wrote based on her romance with Duke— and the novel that causes them all sorts of trouble.**

*An Excerpt from*

## THE WICKED WALLFLOWER

*In the garden*

THOUGH THEY WERE in full view of everyone in the drawing room, they could not be heard, thanks to the French doors that the duke deliberately closed behind them—with an apologetic grin to all the ladies, of course. Not one of whom moved, other than to obtain a better view of the unfathomable sight of Emma strolling arm in arm with London's Most Eligible Bachelor Of All Time Ever.

She inhaled deeply, discovering the duke's manly scent of fresh linen and wool mingling with the fragrant flowers of the garden. She exhaled slowly. None of this could be real. At any second now, everything would return to normal, or perhaps even worse.

What cursed person had sent the letter? And heaven's above, what was the duke actually doing here, in her garden, his muscled arm linked with hers?

"It seems we are engaged," Blake remarked casually. As if he were only commenting on the weather. As if they were acquainted, and not complete strangers to each other.

"We did nothing to dispel the rumors," Emma replied.

"Rumors? It was printed in the paper."

"Very well, libel," Emma corrected. "But you could still cry off."

She so kindly gave him the opportunity to live down to her expectations. She found herself holding her breath and glancing up at his impossibly handsome profile while she still had the opportunity to do so.

"Do you not want to marry me?" he asked, as if that had anything to do with it. She had not even considered it.

"Your Grace, I don't even know you."

"A minor detail, and one that is easily remedied." Then he glanced down at her with dark eyes and a suggestive smile. "It would be a pleasure to become better acquainted."

He said this, of course, in a manner that left no doubt as to what sort of pleasure or acquaintance he intended. Emma felt her temperature rising, but would not allow herself to engage in his flirtations. She did not want to be swept away upon some flight of fancy, only to come crashing down when the world inevitably restored itself to the proper order in which the likes of him did not engage with the likes of her.

"I should think our lack of acquaintance is a significant detail, actually," she said. "And one not necessarily in need of a remedy."

The duke paused, and turned to face her. She was struck by the perfection of him. She, who had a crooked smile and plain brown hair and perfectly fine features, could not even imagine possessing such beauty as he.

He didn't even seem aware of how utterly handsome he was, and how it made a girl lose her wits around him.

Emma resolved then and there that she would be immune to the Ashbrooke Affect. She would not be yet another simpering, silly girl who flung herself at his feet. While the world as she'd always known it no longer made sense, Emma stubbornly clung to one truth: the likes of her and the likes of Ashbrooke could not belong together. Therefore, there was no point in acting prettily, as if she could 1) suddenly learn to flirt and 2) as if something would come of it.

No, she wanted Benedict and their little townhouse full of books and babies. She wanted to be with a man who was safe, steady and constant.

"I have a proposal for you," the duke said, clasping her hands. His were large, warm and he scandalously did not wear gloves.

"Another one?"

He laughed, a rich, low, velvety sound, and she was overwhelmed by a flush of heat and pleasure just from the vibrations of it. Though she may have suffered a fleeting sensation that might have been the infamous Ashbrooke Effect, she would perish before admitting it.

They did not belong together. She would do well to remember that.

She promptly forgot as he dropped to one knee.

"What in blazes are you doing?" Emma tried to yank him up to stand, but he held onto her hand firmly. She glanced, panicked, at the group of ladies pressed up against the drawing room window.

The duke remained on one knee, peering at her with an earnest look in his eyes and a hint of a smile on his lips.

"Emily, will you marry me?"

"Are you mad?"

"Smile, darling, they're watching," he murmured.

"Your Grace, we both know this betrothal announcement is . . . a joke. It's not real," she told him. That much had to be said. She owed him that.

"I'm not an idiot, Emma," Blake said frankly, though he smiled as if he were in the midst of a proposal, because he remained on bended knee. "I know that someone with a warped sense of humor or twisted idea of vengeance thought it'd be an amusing prank to announce an engagement between two people who have never met. I don't know what kind of unhinged person would do such a thing."

Emma declined to offer further intelligence on the matter. In fact, she vowed to take the truth of the letter's authors to her grave, just as she vowed to seek revenge upon the horrible person who had actually sent it.

"But now I am proposing in truth. I beg you to say yes," he said so solemnly, she almost considered it. She narrowed her eyes, finding this proposal highly suspicious. She'd wager that when the duke awoke this morning, he didn't even know she was alive. And yet here he was, on bended knee insanely proposing that they marry. He could not be serious.

Perhaps he was insane.

Or perhaps the duke had an ulterior motive. While she did not want to be unwed at Lady Penelope's ball, she also didn't want to throw her life away on a whim to suit an addled aristocrat.

She wanted Benedict. The man she loved. The man who actually and truly knew her.

*Benedict! Where was he? Why was he not here?* Probably because he thought her engaged to a man who towered above him in rank. He probably thought she lied and deceived him, too. Which is why she had to end this farce and explain to Benedict the truth. They could then elope and live simply in the country or in that townhouse on Brook Street.

That was the happily-ever-after of which she dreamed. She would not be the plain and forgotten wife of an infamous scoundrel, notorious rogue and dashing duke.

"Thank you, Your Grace. But I cannot accept."

She, a lowly, impoverished wallflower on her fourth season had just done the unthinkable: refused a wealthy duke. She must have gone mad.

In spite of her rejection, Ashbrooke just smiled. Then he stood, towering over her, and he gently lowered his mouth to hers and brushed his lips across her own. It was only an instant, but she felt sparks.

She felt the snap and sizzle of a fire flickering to life.

And she became aware that she'd never felt that with Benedict.

A lot could happen in an instant.

"What are you about?" she asked, dazed. He gently pushed a lock of hair away from her cheek. It was the affectionate caress of a lover.

"A kiss to celebrate our betrothal. For making me the happiest man in the world when you said yes."

"I did no such thing," she declared. Good God, the man was daft. All beauty and no brains.

"According to that dozen of gossips in there," he said, inclining his head and never once taking his eyes off her face, "you just did."

"They couldn't hear me—" she said as the truth dawned. He wasn't daft at all. He was devious and she had just fallen neatly into his trap.

"But they could see," he murmured, devastatingly.

They could see that he had proposed on one knee—again, presumably. They could see that he had kissed her. They would never, ever, ever, ever, ever consider that Emma would refuse him.

Emma touched her fingers to her lips. They burned. Still burned. One fleeting kiss in the garden, and she was betrayed. Ruined. Like Judas and Jesus. One fleeting kiss and the duke of Ashbrooke had robbed her of her hopes, her dreams.

They were as good as married now. There would be no more Benedict, no little townhouse. She'd be the lonely duchess, married to a man far more attractive than she, and always the subject of cruel whispers. What does he see in her? She could just imagine the gossip columns: *To the surprise of no one, the duke of Ashbrooke continues his rakehell ways despite his marriage to the buxom bluestocking who at least has books to comfort her.*

It was not the life she had planned, nor was it a life she wished for.

Emma would never forgive him that.

*I am a wallflower,* she wanted to protest. *I love another.* But she was a smart girl. Thus, Emma knew none of that mattered anymore. Not after a duke kissed her in the garden, in full view of at least two dozen of London's greatest gossips. In a way, that was more official than actually signing the marriage contracts.

"Welcome to happily ever after," Ashbrooke said, linking his arm with hers. "Allow me to explain."

"Please do," she said in a strangled whisper. Rage had a way of tangling up words.

"You are one of London's Least Likely," the duke said smoothly and she bit down on her lip.

"Really, you are going to start with that? I had heard you were considered an expert seducer. Clearly, that rumor is an outrageous exaggeration."

"As you pointed out, I have, over the years, acquired a reputation as something a rake."

"That's an understatement," she said. "One might say a ruthless scoundrel, a notorious libertine, a horrible jackanapes."

"Think, Emma, of how this betrothal could serve each other," Ashbrooke said, keeping is voice even and his grasp on her secure. "My reputation would be mended by an engagement with a respectable girl."

"Words every girl wants to hear to describe herself.

Really, I cannot fathom how you got your reputation for being such a seductive charmer."

"On my arm, you will become a sensation," Ashbrooke said plainly. "Let us face the facts: No one noticed you before, but everyone will want you now. When you cry off in a few weeks, I shall be inconsolable and take an extended visit away from London and you shall have your pick of suitors."

Hope flickered. Then died.

"I'm not sure the world works like that," Emma said. The world was a different place for those that were not charming, powerful, wealthy dukes. "I would be seen as The Duke Of Ashbrooke's jilted fiancé. Hardly the stuff of other men's dreams."

"That's where you are wrong," he stated flatly.

"I knew you would be arrogant," Emma muttered "I am not pleased to be proven correct."

"It's not arrogance, it's the facts," he said with an impatient sigh.

"Why should I not cry off now? Because I really would like to." Emma glared stubbornly up at him. She detected a hint of a smile, a spark of appreciation in his eyes. She scowled all the more.

"You could jilt me now," he said slowly. "Even though two dozen women are already spinning stories of our whirlwind romance and romantic stroll in the garden. Everyone will think this was just a joke. You will be no better off than before. You'd be worse, even. And if you cried off now, we wouldn't have the fortune."

Her breath caught. Hope flickered again.

"What fortune?"

"My dear aunt Agatha is holding a house party at which she shall determine who will inherit her enormous fortune. She is also ancient."

Hope flickered again, and a flame burst forth. And then it died again.

"Allow me to confirm that I am understanding you correctly," Emma said slowly. "You would like us to pose as a betrothed couple to swindle your wealthy, elderly aunt out of her fortune."

"It does sound nefarious when phrased like that, I grant you," he said, grinning. "But it's all part of The Fortune Games, a mad scheme of Agatha's own creation."

"Ah yes, Lady Agatha Grey's Fortune Games. I have heard the most intriguing things about it. You have never won, have you?" Emma asked, eyes narrowed. Why should I team up with a loser? She didn't dare say it, but she hoped her expression conveyed it.

"With you as my blushing bride I would," he said, so confidently. "We would."

"And then I may jilt you and keep my portion of the reward?"

"If that's what you wish," he replied, eyeing her curiously. He obviously could not fathom that she might not with to be with him. She was not at all sorry to provide this rude awakening to him.

"It is exactly what I wish," she said firmly. It was her one and only one chance to still attain the life she dreamt of. So long as she won the fortune and didn't do something ridiculous, like fall for the duke.

"Is there anything you wish to tell me, Emma? Is there another man? Are you in a particular condition?"

"We might pose as a happily betrothed couple, but you should know my heart belongs to someone else," she said, oddly delighted that he thought she, London's Least Likely To Misbehave, could possibly have gotten herself ruined or in a particular condition.

"So you'll say yes," he repeated.

"Apparently I already have," she remarked dryly. For the fortune. For Benedict.

Ashbrooke broke into a smile, a grin of such pure happiness. The force of such radiant, beautiful joy hit her like a runaway carriage pulled by a half dozen charging stallions.

The duke wrapped his arms around her, swept her off her feet and whirled her around—right there, in the garden, with all the gossips of London watching. And then he kissed her—another swift brush of his warm, firm mouth against hers. She thought of fireworks and a strange feeling of warmth and desire surging through her. She did not think of Benedict.

She thought of the Ashbrooke Affect.

It was real. It knocked her breath away, along with her wits.

"Pack your bags, Emma Wallflower," Ashbrooke said in a happy, laughing voice. "We have a house party to attend and a dowager to charm out of her fortune."

## *About the Author*

Maya Rodale began reading romance novels in college at her mother's insistence and it wasn't long before she was writing her own. Maya is now the author of multiple historical and contemporary romances. She lives in New York City with her darling dog and a rogue of her own.

Please visit her at www.mayarodale.com.

[redacted]